"I think the _____
Tye," Susannah said unevenly. "That's why he's so dangerous."

Just for a moment she would have sworn she saw something flash behind those eyes—something that could have been pain.

"What's that expression about giving a dog a bad name?"

Without seeming to move at all, suddenly Tye had lessened the distance between them to no more than a few inches. Behind her, Susannah felt the hard edge of the counter pressing into her back.

"Give a dog a bad name and he'll bite?" she ventured.

"That's it." He bent his head, obliterating the last of her precious buffer zone. "You can call me off anytime, Suze," he said, his tone velvety. "But maybe you don't want to. Maybe after a lifetime of putting the devil behind you, just this once you'd like to be tempted...."

Dear Harlequin Intrigue Reader,

We've got an intoxicating lineup crackling with passion and peril that's guaranteed to lure you to Harlequin Intrigue this month!

Danger and desire abound in *As Darkness Fell*—the first of two installments in Joanna Wayne's HIDDEN PASSIONS: Full Moon Madness companion series. In this stark, seductive tale, a rugged detective will go to extreme lengths to safeguard a feisty reporter who is the object of a killer's obsession. Then temptation and terror go hand in hand in *Lone Rider Bodyguard* when Harper Allen launches her brand-new miniseries, MEN OF THE DOUBLE B RANCH.

Will revenge give way to sweet salvation in *Undercover Avenger* by Rita Herron? Find out in the ongoing NIGHTHAWK ISLAND series. If you're searching high and low for a thrilling romantic suspense tale that will also satisfy your craving for adventure—you'll be positively riveted by *Bounty Hunter Ransom* from Kara Lennox's CODE OF THE COBRA.

Just when you thought it was safe to sleep with the lights off…*Guardian of her Heart* by Linda O. Johnston—the latest offering in our BACHELORS AT LARGE promotion—will send shivers down your spine. And don't let down your guard quite yet. Lisa Childs caps off a month of spine-tingling suspense with a gripping thriller about a madman bent on revenge in *Bridal Reconnaissance*. You won't want to miss this unforgettable debut of our new DEAD BOLT promotion.

Here's hoping these smoldering Harlequin Intrigue novels will inspire some romantic dreams of your own this Valentine's Day!

Enjoy,

Denise O'Sullivan
Senior Editor
Harlequin Intrigue

LONE RIDER BODYGUARD

HARPER ALLEN

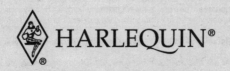

TORONTO • NEW YORK • LONDON
AMSTERDAM • PARIS • SYDNEY • HAMBURG
STOCKHOLM • ATHENS • TOKYO • MILAN • MADRID
PRAGUE • WARSAW • BUDAPEST • AUCKLAND

ISBN 0-373-22754-X

LONE RIDER BODYGUARD

Copyright © 2004 by Sandra Hill

This edition published by arrangement with Harlequin Books S.A.

® and TM are trademarks of the publisher. Trademarks indicated with
® are registered in the United States Patent and Trademark Office, the
Canadian Trade Marks Office and in other countries.

Visit us at www.eHarlequin.com

Printed in U.S.A.

ABOUT THE AUTHOR

Harper Allen lives in the country in the middle of a hundred acres of maple trees with her husband, Wayne, six cats, four dogs—and a very nervous cockatiel at the bottom of the food chain. For excitement she and Wayne drive to the nearest village and buy jumbo bags of pet food. She believes in love at first sight because it happened to her.

Books by Harper Allen

HARLEQUIN INTRIGUE

*The Avengers
†Men of the Double B Ranch

Don't miss any of our special offers. Write to us at the following address for information on our newest releases.

Harlequin Reader Service
U.S.: 3010 Walden Ave., P.O. Box 1325, Buffalo, NY 14269
Canadian: P.O. Box 609, Fort Erie, Ont. L2A 5X3

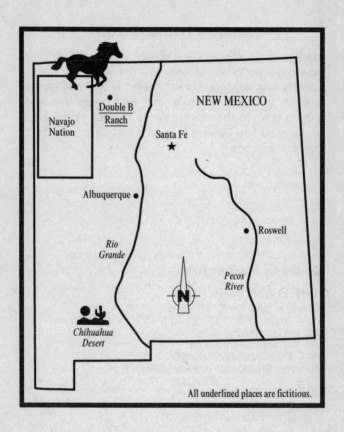

NEW MEXICO

Navajo
Nation

Double B
Ranch

Santa Fe ★

Albuquerque ●

Roswell ●

Rio
Grande

Pecos
River

N

Chihuahua
Desert

All underlined places are fictitious.

CAST OF CHARACTERS

Susannah Bird—On the run from her husband's killers, can she trust the brooding stranger who helps deliver her son and find refuge at the Double B Ranch?

Tyler Adams—The bodyguard with a past will take on any risk to protect Susannah and her newborn son—but has he put his own heart in danger?

Del Hawkins—The Vietnam vet runs the Double B Ranch, a reform camp for teens in trouble—as Tye Adams had once been. But is the ranch still a refuge for those in danger…or a deadly trap?

Alice Tahe—The Navajo matriarch claims she sees an evil she calls Skinwalker threatening the Double B…and Susannah's baby.

Vincent Rosario—The two-bit crook has a grudge against Del. He doesn't care if he has to destroy a young mother and her child to carry out his plan.

Michael Saranno—The mobster may have had a reason for having Susannah's ex-husband eliminated, but what about her and her child?

Paul Johnson and *Kevin Bradley*—Can Tye trust the Double B hired hands to keep danger away from Susannah?

Daniel Bird, John MacLeish, Zeke Harmond—Along with Del Hawkins, they were the members of the original Double B—Beta Beta Force, a covert ops organization in Vietnam that was disbanded in tragedy.

To Saint Martha and the menagerie

Chapter One

Whoever she was, she was in trouble.

A woman's breathing, harsh and edged, sliced the sudden silence as Tyler Adams cut the engine of the big Harley and brought it to a halt ahead of the sedan by the side of the highway. He still couldn't see her, but as he strode back to the car the pain-filled gasps came faster. Guilt flickered through him.

He almost hadn't stopped. Hell, he'd kept going for another mile or so before his conscience had gotten the better of him and he'd turned back to investigate. It hadn't been much—just a blinding sparkle coming from the far side of the sedan as he'd passed it—but the only reason he could think of for the sparkle he'd glimpsed was that the car's back door had been open a little. Muttering under his breath, he'd turned the Harley around.

He'd been right, the back door was open. Protruding from it were two slim legs. Two bare feet dug into the hard-packed New Mexico dirt, their heels lifted and the tendons of their high arches standing out against the fine white road dust covering them. Swiftly he began to walk around the open door to get a look at the rest of her, and as he did the gasps turned into a grunt.

"Stay right there, mister." The words sounded forced. "I—I've got a gun."

Dammit, she's been attacked. Even as he froze, the sickened thought tore through his mind. She'd been assaulted and she thought he was the bastard who'd done this to her, come back for a second sadistic round.

Tye suddenly wished he was a couple of inches shorter than six feet, instead of a few over, and a little less bulky, less broad-shouldered. Intimidating worked in his job—he'd built up the bodyguard and protection firm he headed into the agency of choice for nervous celebrities, partially on the strength of the don't-screw-with-me impression he apparently projected—but she didn't need big and intimidating right now.

"I'm not here to hurt you, lady." The ground between her raised heels was darkly wet. *Blood,* he thought with icy anger. "Let me help you back onto the seat so I can drive you to a hospital."

The gun thing had probably been a bluff. He stepped past the open door and got his first clear look at her.

The gun thing hadn't been a bluff. She was holding a massive revolver in both hands, and at this distance if she pulled the trigger he'd be a goner even before he hit the ground. But the damn gun wasn't important.

She was wearing a summery dress, white with a pattern of red cherries. There were three red buttons on the opened bodice, one of them hanging by a thread, and the ripe swell of her breasts was almost fully exposed. In the hollow between them her skin was slick with sweat.

Her hair was the pale brown of buckwheat honey, deeper by a shade than his own dark blond. It hung in damp strands to her shoulders. The hands holding the revolver were propped up on the enormous curve of her belly.

She was pregnant. Make that *very* pregnant, Tye told himself hollowly. She was so pregnant that any time now she wouldn't be pregnant anymore. Any time now the baby inside her was going to start coming out.

He saw her slitted eyes lose focus for a moment, heard her breath whistle between her gritted teeth. Slowly she exhaled.

"I suspect for the next little while I'm goin' to be too busy to be able to worry about you, mister," she said softly. "This isn't anything I ever thought I'd find myself doing, but you people left me no choice."

He'd told himself the damn gun wasn't important, but he'd been wrong about that, too. The explosion split the dusty silence like a thunderclap.

He couldn't remember actually making the decision to hit the ground, Tyler thought a second later. But apparently he had and apparently he almost hadn't been fast enough. The slashed shoulder of his leather jacket was evidence of that. *Losing your edge, buddy,* he told himself tightly. *Better start getting out in the field again, sharpen up those reflexes.*

"You shouldn't have done that, mister." The soft voice shook. "I was going for a wing shot, but if you'd jumped the other way this whole thing would have turned out bad for the both of us. I've got no desire to bring my baby into the world with blood on my—oh!''

The abrupt exclamation ended in a small gasp, and something about the vulnerability of that noise drove all caution from his mind. Quickly he got to his feet.

Her eyes were squeezed shut and the gun was beside her on the floor of the car. Tye seized his chance.

''Whoever you think I am, you're wrong, lady,'' he said tersely. ''You need to get to a delivery room, and fast. Where are the car keys?''

''I guess the part Granny Lacey used to call the rest-and-be-thankful stage is over.'' Her voice was thready. ''The car broke down, mister. Did I make a mistake about you?''

''I made a couple about you, so I guess we're even,'' he answered briefly. ''Just tell me if I've got it right. Someone's after you, this junker isn't going anywhere and you're about to have a baby. That about it?'' At her nod he went on, hoping he sounded calmer than he felt. ''How long have you been in labor?''

''My water broke about half an hour after the car died,'' she murmured. Which explained the dampness of the ground between her heels, he thought in relief. ''I'm pretty sure I'm fully dilated now. My body's telling me it's time to start pushing.''

Tye could still remember the first foal he'd watched being born. Del Hawkins had rousted him, Connor, Riggs and Jess from their beds, only waiting long enough for them to pull on jeans and boots. The four of them had exchanged furious glances, but after a week at the Double B they'd known better than to flat-out confront the wheelchair-bound ex-Marine.

He'd been a tough and surly sixteen-year-old at the

time, Tye reflected. He'd thought nothing could get to him. But at the sight of that wobbly foal scrambling up on ridiculously long legs he'd realized there was a lump in his throat. In the glow of the lantern he'd seen the others averting their faces, too.

That night had been a turning point, but he wasn't sure it qualified him for this.

"There's a plaid carpetbag on the front seat. I need the newspaper that's in it."

Her top lip was dewed with moisture and she'd closed her eyes again. The pain had to be bad, Tye thought. It had her talking crazy—although stress and fear might have something to do with that, too. Who was after her? An abusive husband, despite the fact she wore no wedding band? That seemed unlikely, since from her few cryptic remarks he'd received the impression there was more than one person looking for her, but his questions would have to go unanswered for now. Unzipping his jacket and slinging it onto the roof of the car, he bent down beside her.

"You don't want to read the paper. If there's something in that carpetbag I could use to boil water in I could get a fire going."

"Newspapers are the most sterile thing you can use in an emergency like this, mister. I need it to cover the car seat for when my little one comes out." She opened her eyes, and for the first time he saw they were almost the same color as her hair—a clear honey-gold, but with a flash of unexpected humor in them. "My Granny Lacey was a midwife, and I started attending birthings with her when I was just a teeny girl myself. I'd be beholden to you for any help you could give me, though."

She bit her lip, the smile in her eyes disappearing. "But no matter how far along I am, if a car with out-of-state plates slows down you grab ahold of that gun. I can't explain now, but it appears someone's looking to bring harm to me and my baby. I—I figured you were working with them," she added. "I'm real sorry for shooting at you, mister."

"The name's Adams. Tyler Adams."

He reached over the seat for the carpetbag, oddly glad for any excuse to take his gaze from that steady golden one and surprised to find himself feeling so off balance. It was the situation, not the woman, he thought. It couldn't be the woman, because women never made him feel off balance.

"Susannah Bird. I'm pleased to make your acquaintance, Mr. Ad—"

Her heels were no longer dug into the earth, but braced on the edge of the seat. As he laid another section of newsprint beneath her upraised knees, her words broke off and the next moment he felt his wrist being held in an unexpectedly strong grip.

"This is it."

The soft tones had been replaced by an effort-filled mutter. Her bent legs opened, the cherry-patterned skirt that till now had provided a tent-like decorum slipping up her thighs. Automatically he moved his gaze to her face, feeling unexpected heat mount in his own, and found himself meeting a fierce honey-gold glare.

"This isn't no time to stand on ceremony, Tye. And if you're the squeamish kind, I'll thank you to leave me to handle this myself," she ground out between cracked lips.

She was right, he thought, angry with himself. Even though he'd only met Susannah Bird moments ago, even though what she was about to go through would leave no room for modesty, it was the most basic, natural act in the world. And although there'd been a more immediate reason for his returning to New Mexico after all these years, there was no denying that in the back of his mind he'd also had the vague thought that in the place where his life had been turned around once, he might again find some kind of renewal, some kind of grounding.

Before he'd even reached his destination he'd stumbled onto the opportunity to help bring new life into the world. How much more grounded could he get?

"You don't get rid of me as easily as that," he said, the curtness in his voice not directed at her. "I'm no Granny Lacey, but I'm all you've got. I'm staying."

Incredibly, the parched lips curved into a smile even as the harsh panting continued and her brows knitted together. For a second her grip on him slackened and he reached into the carpetbag by his feet.

Despite the climbing morning heat, the bottle of water he'd noticed was still cool. Rummaging a little deeper, he came up with a neatly-folded washcloth. Gently he ran the dampened cloth over her moisture-beaded forehead, her dry lips. Through her lashes she shot him a grateful glance.

"Feels…good," she managed. "Baby…crowning yet, Tye?"

Crowning? What the hell was crowning? he thought in confusion, replacing the bottle's cap with fingers that felt suddenly thick and clumsy.

Whatever it is, there's only one place you're going

to be able to see if it's happening, a caustic voice inside his head said. *Stop warming the bench and get into the game here.*

Tye hunkered down at the side of the vehicle, and not a moment too soon, he immediately realized. Crowning meant he was the first human being to lay eyes on this new little person who was emerging into the world.

"Aahh!!"

The guttural cry sounded as if it was being wrenched from Susannah's throat. She'd propped herself up on her elbows, her head thrown back and every tendon in her neck standing out in rigid relief. She cried again, and he could see the agony etched on her contorted features.

"You're doing fine, Suze," he rasped, knowing as he spoke how inadequate his words were. "You're doing great. Keep pushing, honey."

About to check on the baby's progress again, out of the corner of his eye he saw a large, cream-colored blur speed by. *Where did that come from?* he thought in sharp alarm, flicking an automatic glance at the revolver on the floor. The Cadillac receded into the distance without slowing, and he frowned.

She'd been a woman alone on the road, in an unreliable vehicle and with a baby due any time. She might have glimpsed the same car at different gas stations along the way, and out of that concocted a fearful scenario that had grown bigger in her mind with each passing mile. When she'd been at her most vulnerable he'd come along—a jeans-and-leather-clad—

His heart stopped. It started up again, crashing so hard against his ribs it felt as if it was trying to escape.

"His head's out, Suze," he said hoarsely. Without conscious thought, he put a swift hand beneath the small skull to support it, just as he heard another incoherent cry issue from her throat.

When he'd been fifteen he'd broken his leg wiping out in a curve on a borrowed motorcycle without a license. During his year at the Double B Ranch he'd been thrown from Chorizo, a hammer-headed Appaloosa gelding Hawkins had expressly forbidden them to ride. Last year he'd taken a bullet in the ribs.

He'd figured he knew what endurance was. But he was a male. He had no idea what toughing it out meant, Tye realized now.

The baby was coming out on its side. Instinctively he lowered the fragile head a fraction, and an incredibly tiny shoulder popped into view. Again acting on instinct and hoping desperately that his instincts were right, he raised his supporting hands slightly.

The bottom shoulder emerged, so suddenly that for one frantic moment his cautious hold almost slipped.

"Turn—turn him on his back," Susannah gasped. "Bag. Swabs. His nose—"

The little sucker was slippery, Tye thought disjointedly. This was like trying to hang on to a wet football in the rain, and one-handed it was even harder. Groping around in the bag by his feet, his fingers came into contact with a package.

"Cotton swabs," he muttered. "Touchdown."

There was some kind of gunk in the little guy's nose and in the tiny mouth. Presumably the gunk had to come out.

"Of course, you could be a girl," he said under his breath. He willed his hand to stop shaking, and swabbed at the minute, perfectly-formed nostrils, the goldfish lips. "If you are, no offense, okay? But until we know for sure I'm going to think of you as a—"

"Granny Lacey, *help* me!"

Even as he heard Susannah's high-pitched plea to a woman who wasn't there, Tye felt the small body slide completely into his hands, and frantically he adjusted his hold on—on *him,* he thought, feeling a grin spreading across his features. It was a boy. They'd had a boy!

"He looks just like me," he said stupidly. "Just like me, Suze." He met her pain-sheened gaze, unable to stop smiling despite the moisture he could feel prickling at the back of his eyes. "I mean he's a boy," he amended. "We—you've got a brand-new baby boy."

"Is he breathing okay, Tye?" Concern overrode the fatigue in her tone. "Rub his back."

Apparently it wasn't like the movies. You didn't introduce them to the world with a hearty slap on the rump. With infinite care he rubbed the little back and the crumpled lips pursed out, as if they were trying to blow a bubble. The miniscule eyelids squeezed even more tightly shut. A weak cry, more like the mew of a kitten than anything else, came from those crumpled lips.

In the space of a heartbeat—a skipped heartbeat, Tye thought shakily—the kitten-cry became an outraged squall that seemed far too big to have come from such a tiny body.

"Oh, Tye, let me hold him."

Susannah was propped against the back of the car seat, her arms outstretched. Carefully he leaned forward and placed the small squirming body against her opened bodice before standing back and looking down at them.

Her hair hung in strands, her face was still red from her exertions and her bottom lip had either split slightly or she'd sunk her teeth in too deeply and bitten it at some time during the past hour. The cherry-strewn dress would never be presentable again.

She was so beautiful she took his breath away.

Those hazel-gold eyes were luminous with joy as she looked upon her new son for the first time. With no self-consciousness at all, tenderly she shifted the baby in her arms to her breast. As if a switch had been turned off, the crying stopped…and suddenly everything fell into place.

This was what it all came down to, Tye thought—a mother, a baby and a man watching over them. Why hadn't he ever figured it out before?

"I got sterile thread to tie off the cord when the afterbirth comes out," Susannah murmured, not taking her gaze from her son. "But Granny Lacey always said it was best to wait. Isn't he perfect, Tye? Isn't he just the most perfect baby you ever saw?"

"He's better than perfect, Suze."

When had he started calling her that and when had she started calling him Tye? he wondered, before dismissing the question. It didn't matter. All he knew was that it seemed right. Despite the fact that they'd barely touched, he'd never felt closer to any woman in his life.

No ring on her finger doesn't mean she's not married.

A second ago he'd felt as if he'd just drunk a whole

bottle of champagne. His euphoria came crashing down to earth.

He was a stranger who'd happened to be passing by, and the bond he'd thought he sensed between them was all in his imagination. This baby was some other man's son.

"I'm going to name him Daniel, after my daddy." Her voice was ragged with exhaustion. "I'd like his middle name to be Tyler, if that's all right with you. I figure you're a big part of why he's here in my arms, safe and sound."

For a moment Tye couldn't say a word. Then he pulled himself together.

"His father had a bigger part, Susannah. I'm sure he wouldn't want his son bearing a stranger's name instead of his own."

"His father's dead. And since everything else he told me was a lie, I can't even be sure the name I knew him by was real."

She looked away, but not before he saw a shadow cross her features. "I didn't shame myself with Frank Barrett," she said softly. "We were married. But even if he'd lived, I know now he wasn't the type to raise a child—maybe because inside he'd never really grown up himself. I want my son to be proud of the name he bears."

She raised her eyes to his. "My daddy was a man," she said simply. "He stood up for what he believed in, he would have given his life for the ones he loved and whenever he had to make a choice between taking the easy way out or doing what he thought was right, he went with his conscience. I think you're the same kind. I'd take it as a honor if you let me name this little one Daniel Tyler Bird.''

Less than an hour ago that steady gaze holding his had made him feel off balance, Tye thought. But it had been everything else in his life that had been spinning out of control.

Most people would say the baby in her arms had come into this world with the cards stacked against him. He didn't have a father. His mother couldn't be much older than twenty—far too young to take on the responsibility of raising a child alone. He'd been born in the back seat of a broken-down car at the side of a dusty road.

But Daniel Tyler Bird already had everything he would ever need. His young mother had a wisdom far beyond her years, rooted in the values and morals of the family she'd spoken of.

And Daniel Tyler was loved by Susannah Bird.

"The honor's mine, Suze," Tye said huskily. "I'd be proud to have your son carry my name."

"FROM WHAT you described, sounds like both mama and baby came through the whole thing just fine." The gray-haired man wedged between Tyler and the driver on the front seat of the ambulance shot a glance in the direction of Tye's clenched jaw. "Me and Wesley here saw the California plates on that fancy chopper you parked outside my clinic. You in these parts scouting movie locations?"

Tye shook his head. "I'm just here to look up an old friend," he said, not taking his eyes from the highway ahead.

He didn't elaborate. As if sensing his preoccupation, Dr. Jennings let the subject drop, and as he and the driver fell into conversation Tye's thoughts returned to the woman he'd left nearly an hour ago.

Susannah had nodded when he'd told her he saw no choice but to leave her and Danny while he went into Last Chance to get medical help. "That May sun's going to turn this car into an oven, Tye," she'd said, concern darkening her gaze. "You're right, we can't just hope someone's going to come along. Except for you, there hasn't been a vehicle go by the whole time I've been here."

He hadn't corrected her. "I'll be back as soon as I can," he'd promised. "There's nothing else left to tie off or take care of or—"

Her laughter had been low. "No, that's it. Granny Lacey couldn't have done a better job of cutting the cord." She'd hesitated. "I—I'm glad it was you who stopped, Tye. And not just because of how you helped Daniel and me."

He hadn't told Doc Jennings anything close to the truth, Tyler thought now. He hadn't come back to Last Chance to look up Hawkins, he'd come because Del had called him with an urgent and unprecedented request for his help. But even before Del had called he'd been trying to find some excuse to make the trip back here to New Mexico, because for the past few years everything he'd worked for, everything he'd thought he wanted out of life, had begun to seem meaningless. And when one day last month he'd looked into his shaving mirror and for a split second had seen the face of his father, he'd felt real fear.

He'd needed answers. He hadn't really been sure what his questions were. But when he'd put Susannah

Bird's newborn son into her arms and she'd given him that glance of purest joy, all his unasked questions and unknown answers had been swept away.

"What fool would throw a jacket onto the side of the road?" Mild as it was, Jennings's quizzical question broke into Tyler's thoughts.

"Tourists." At the wheel, Wesley snorted. "More money than—"

"Turn around." At his terse command, Tye saw the driver and Jennings exchange glances. He spoke again, his tone still sharp. "I think that's my jacket. I left it on the roof of her car."

"I thought you said her vehicle had broken down." As Wesley maneuvered the ambulance onto the hard-baked shoulder and began executing a cautious three-point turn, Jennings frowned. "Besides, a woman who'd just given birth couldn't hop into the front seat and drive off, Adams."

"I know that." Tye felt the knot in his stomach tighten. "But this is where I left her, I'm sure of it."

Unwilling to wait, he opened the ambulance door and jumped out. Sprinting the hundred yards or so back to the discarded leather jacket Jennings had seen, he picked it up.

It was his. High up on the right sleeve was the gaping slash where her bullet had sliced through. At his feet was a darker patch in the parched dust, and on either side of the patch were the shallow impressions where her heels had dug in.

"I can't explain now, but it appears like someone's looking to bring harm to me and my baby...."

Despite the heat, suddenly he felt encased in ice.

He'd left her and Daniel Tyler unprotected. And now they were gone.

Chapter Two

"Do you know what today is, little one?"

Susannah adjusted the flame of the oil lamp on the dresser until the warm glow reflected off the adobe walls just enough to illuminate the two objects hanging on their otherwise unadorned smoothness. One was a large canvas, its jewel-like colors shimmering richly. On the opposite wall hung a plain olive-wood cross. Walking to the handmade cradle by the bed, Susannah bent over her sleeping son.

"You're a whole week old today, starshine," she said softly. "Happy birthday, Daniel Tyler."

She'd made the right decision, she told herself, stroking a fine curl of hair from his delicately veined temple. She and her baby had disappeared without a trace. She'd bought them time, and for now Danny was safe.

That safety had come at a cost.

"I know there's people who don't believe in miracles, Danny, but that's like not believing in rain or puppies or fresh-baked bread," she murmured. "God gives us presents every day. He gave me you. And the day you were born, two more miracles dropped into my life.''

She bit her lip, her gaze darkening. ''One of them was Tyler Adams, the man who made sure you came into this world safely,'' she whispered.

When he grew old enough to ask questions, what would she tell her little boy about the man whose name he bore? she wondered. That even when she'd first laid eyes on him, convinced he was working for the killers who'd been hunting her for the last nine months, she'd thought he was the handsomest man she'd ever seen? That his hair had been the color of burnished gold, his eyes bluer than the sky? That he'd been so tall and broad-shouldered he'd blocked out the sun?

He'd stood there gazing down at her, his perfectly chiselled features remote and unreadable, his skin slightly windburned. Under his unzipped leather jacket she'd seen the white of a T-shirt. There'd been an oil smear high up on one hard cheekbone, and his jeans and boots had been grimy with road dust.

He'd looked dangerous and beautiful at the same time. He'd looked like a picture she'd seen long ago in a children's book of Bible stories, of an angel who'd fallen from grace.

She'd come close to blowing her miracle away with a .38 caliber bullet.

''I could have *killed* him.'' In the quiet room her voice was hoarse with remembered horror. ''He must have thought I was crazy—but still he stayed.''

He'd not only stayed with her, he'd delivered her baby. And when he'd gently put Daniel Tyler into her arms, he'd looked at her as if she was the most beautiful woman he'd ever seen. Unconsciously Susannah pressed her palms to her cheeks, feeling hot color rise under her fingertips. After a minute, the heat subsided and she dropped her hands to her sides.

She had to have imagined that part, she told herself.

"You were the first miracle," she said to the tiny sleeping form in the cradle. "Tye was the second. And Greta was the third."

"As a hard-headed Minnesota Swede, I don't believe in miracles." The comment came from the tall blonde in the doorway. "I certainly don't see myself as one."

Her stride, long-legged and elegant as she approached, was in contrast to the paint-smeared jeans and shirt she wore. Platinum strands escaped the careless braid hanging halfway down her back.

"But if I did, I'd say this angel definitely qualified." Placing a finger on the edge of the cradle, she gave it a gentle push. "I would have liked to have had one just like you, little man. I would have traded everything else for that."

The ice-blond braid swung forward over the denim-clad shoulder. She met Susannah's gaze. "Instead I had ten years on the covers of *Vogue* and *Harper's*, and when I walked away from it all I was free to devote the rest of my life to my painting." Her smile was crooked. "I should be ashamed of myself, crying for the moon."

"But sometimes the moon's so pretty, isn't it?" Unnecessarily Susannah adjusted Danny's blanket again. "Sometimes a body just can't help wishing she could haul it down from the sky and hold on to it for a while."

Greta's cat-green gaze softened. Slinging an arm over Susannah's shoulder, she steered her toward the door. "If it really was the moon either one of us was talking about, the solution would be easy. There's going to be a full one tonight and I thought we could sit out on the *portale* and watch it rise over the desert. White wine for me, guava juice for you," she added, her perfect nose wrinkling.

As they entered the spacious, stone-flagged kitchen, she shot Susannah a glance before opening the refrigerator door. "You still feel guilty about that Adams man, don't you?"

"He did me a kindness." Susannah looked away. "I don't feel right about the way I repaid him."

"You did what you had to." Chunking a couple of cubes of ice into a tall glass, Greta filled it to the brim with pink juice. Pouring a glass of wine for herself, she took a sip. "*Salut,*" she said briefly. "Let's go smell my roses and howl at the moon."

Startled into laughter despite herself, Susannah followed her new friend into the living room. A traditional kiva fireplace and exposed beams on the ceiling were striking focal points, as were the three unframed abstracts hanging on the walls—abstracts, she'd learned from Greta's offhand comments, that would each bring a small fortune if they were ever placed in a New York gallery. Blocks of color danced joyfully across the canvases. Only on second look did a viewer notice the underwashes of dark blues and purples anchoring the backgrounds.

They were like their creator, she reflected. Although she had to be in her forties, Greta Hassell's beauty was still the first thing a stranger would see, but behind that flawless facade was a compassionate woman with her own hidden pain.

Tye had been gone less than ten minutes when the pickup had pulled over and the slim blonde had gotten out. Her perfect features had paled in shock as she'd taken in the situation—Susannah, her obviously newborn baby at her breast, freezing in the act of grabbing for the revolver at her feet as she realized the newcomer was a woman. The blonde's lips had tightened.

"You're in trouble," she'd said shortly. "And your baby should get out of this heat. I'm taking you to my place."

Automatically Susannah had started to explain the situation. Then she'd stopped, her gaze going to her son.

"I—I need to disappear," she'd said after a moment, her tone low and rapid. "Disappear completely—right down to this no-good vehicle that stranded me here. If you can help me do that I'd be obliged, ma'am."

"There's a tow-hitch on the back of my truck." The emerald eyes had narrowed to slits, but Susannah had seen faint humor in them. "The deal is you tell me what this is all about when you and your baby are rested up." The woman had leaned into the sedan, one arm going around Susannah's shoulders to help her up. "And call me Greta, not ma'am, sweetie."

Just like that they'd become friends, Susannah thought, entering the miniature courtyard—what Greta called the *portale*—attached to the house. Wrought-iron gates set into the enclosing adobe walls kept the outside world at bay, the walls themselves pierced

here and there with small openings. Inside each opening sat a small flickering candle in a votive holder.

"If your little guy wakes up we'll hear him easily
enough." Greta set Daniel's baby monitor on the
glass-topped table, two tiny lines between her brows.
"You know I've been careful not to buy Danny's diapers and supplies in Last Chance, Susannah, but
when I ran into town yesterday to get turpentine I kept
my ears open. No one was talking about a woman and
a baby going missing."

"Maybe after Tye sent the ambulance to get me he
decided to continue on his journey instead of waiting
around. Heaven knows he didn't owe me any more of
his time." Susannah looked toward the house, her
glance going to the window of Daniel's room. "I
guess it wouldn't be the first time the paramedics went
out on a call that didn't pan out, so they wouldn't have
seen any need to raise a hue and cry about it. But that
doesn't change the fact I did him a wrong, Greta."

The other woman hesitated. When she spoke again
she seemed to be choosing her words with care. "I
didn't hear any gossip about strangers poking around,
either," she said quietly. "Tell me—how sure are you
that someone's after you?"

"As sure as I am of the fact that Frank Barrett was
killed," Susannah said flatly. "I identified his dead
body, Greta. And a few weeks after I had him laid to
rest I saw the owner of the diner where I worked killed
by a bullet meant for me."

Restlessly she stood. Through the iron lace of the
gates the moon Greta had promised hung, full and
orange, over the desert. "I just don't know who's after

me or why, which is why every time I've gone to the police I sound like a crazy wom—''

"What is it?" Greta's glance went to the baby monitor at Susannah's quickly indrawn breath.

"Not Danny." Susannah shook her head. "Someone's coming. Were you expecting company?"

Greta was already standing, but as the headlights that had caught Susannah's attention came closer her posture relaxed. "I know better than ever to expect Del Hawkins. Every so often the man simply shows up, and I'm fool enough to run into his arms when he does," she said dryly. "That's partly what was behind our little tiff last week just before he left—although he's back a day earlier than I thought he'd be."

She shrugged. "But I've bored you with that story more than once, sweetie. Do you want to meet my tough old mustang or would you feel better if he didn't know you were here? You can trust him to keep his mouth closed about seeing you," she added, her eyes still on the approaching truck.

He was the reason Greta had never married, and why she'd taken up residence in this remote chunk of New Mexico when she'd decided to concentrate on her painting. If only for those reasons it would be interesting to see just what kind of a man he was, Susannah thought. But even if he and Greta had been no more than acquaintances, his arrival still would have been momentous.

Because if he was the Del Hawkins she'd been looking for, her twenty-five-hundred-mile journey had just come to an end.

Her palms felt suddenly damp. Surreptitiously she pressed them against her thighs.

"Granny Lacey used to say two catbirds sound real sweet singing together, but as soon as a third one shows up the harmony's gone." Her smile felt wobbly. "I'm near ready for my bed, and I suspect my little mister's going to have me up again in a few hours anyway."

Granny Lacey had also said that not telling the whole truth was as good as a lie, Susannah thought, making her way into the house. That one she didn't completely hold with.

"If your great-granny was still alive she'd say I was sliding down that slippery slope real quick, starshine," she murmured to Daniel as she bent over his cradle. "But your mama had to think of something. You'd think nine whole months would have been time enough to prepare myself, but I guess I wasn't as ready as I thought. Besides, there's a chance it might not be him."

She lifted her head, her brows drawing together in a frown as she heard the solid-sounding thunks of not one, but both of the truck's doors being slammed shut. Del had brought a friend. Even if her hasty withdrawal had been for the sole purpose of allowing Greta a few minutes of privacy it would have been all for nothing, anyway.

"Someone should give that fool male a slap," she muttered in momentary distraction, stepping to the screened window and looking out at the candle-and-moonlit patio. As she gazed at the man leaning forward to plant a casual kiss on Greta's slightly parted lips, any last doubts about his identity fled.

He was the Lieutenant Hawkins she'd grown up hearing so much about from her grandmother—the

man her father had served under during a long-ago
and terrible war, one of only two men Daniel Bird had
sworn he would trust with his life. Del had lost both
legs in Vietnam and although Greta had told her he'd
been liberated from a wheelchair ten years ago when
he'd been fitted with prosthetic limbs, the cane he was
holding in his left hand was obviously necessary to
his balance.

"But you're still a fine-looking man, aren't you?"
she said under her breath, watching as Hawkins lightly
touched Greta's hair before turning to introduce his
companion. "And in love with her, if the look on your
face is anything to go by. So why don't you—"

Susannah froze in shock. Her eyes widened painfully as she stared at the stranger standing with Del
Hawkins and Greta.

Except he wasn't a stranger, she thought faintly. He
was a fallen angel, and even while he reached for
Greta's extended hand his attention was fixed on
something on the table.

Tyler Adams raised his eyes from the baby monitor,
his gaze encompassing the courtyard and then going
to the house itself. In the light from the candles the
sweep of his lashes cut shadows on the hard ridges of
his cheekbones.

And at that instant the night exploded in gunfire.

"Get down!"

There was no way he could see her—but incredibly,
Tye's hoarse shout seemed directed at her. Susannah
could have sworn his eyes locked desperately on hers
before he turned swiftly to his companions.

Hawkins had already started to act, one muscled
forearm shooting forward to knock Greta out of the

line of fire coming from the openings in the wall
where the votive candles had been moments ago. Even
as his arm made contact with the blonde, Susannah
saw her slam against him, as if some invisible fist had
driven into her chest with enough force to lift her off
her feet. Del's stricken voice rose above the cacoph-
ony of gunfire.

"Greta!"

As she slumped against his chest he dropped his
cane and took her whole weight with him. His knees
crashed onto the brick of the patio but, showing no
reaction to the pain, he pulled her closer, his arms
wrapping around her as if to shield her with his own
flesh and bone.

Of course he hadn't reacted to the pain. He hadn't
felt any. The last time Del Hawkins's knees had felt
pain had been over thirty years ago in a Mekong Delta
swamp, Susannah reminded herself. Even that long-
ago agony, terrible as it must have been, couldn't have
contorted his features with the anguish she now saw
carved into them.

Wrenching free from the paralysis gripping her, she
whirled from the window and ran to the cradle. As
she bent over it Danny started to scream, his tiny fingers bunched into fists, his eyes wide with shock.

"I'm here, starshine. Mama's here." Scooping him
into her arms, with shaking fingers she wrapped his
blanket tightly around him. Terrified blue eyes stared
into hers, and his screams became louder.

A terrible anger rose up in her, hot and clear, and
her gaze swung to the olive-wood cross, a stark black
silhouette against the shadowed wall.

"He's only a baby, Lord!" Her protest was harshly

agonized. "And that woman outside opened her home to me out of the goodness of her heart. Why are You letting this happen to us?"

The cross swam in front of her burning eyes. It seemed to waver and grow larger, and all of a sudden it was no longer a symbol but two splintered timbers crudely affixed together and set up on a lonely hill, the nine long nails pounded into it put there by human hands, not divine.

It wavered, and once again came into focus.

"I—I'm sorry," Susannah whispered. "Men brought this evil to us, I know. But I can't let it touch my son."

She looked down at the baby in her arms. Bringing her face close to the frightened red one peeping from the blankets, gently she pressed a kiss to Danny's flushed forehead. His screams subsided into a hiccuping sob.

"The man I named you for is out there protecting you, little one. I wish I could do something to help him, but you're my first responsibility. We'll just have to pray he stays safe."

On the dresser by the now-extinguished oil lamp was her purse. She reached for it with her free hand, slinging its strap bandolier-style across her chest.

"Your mama's going to get you out of here, starshine. And Lord help me, if I have to use this to do it I will."

The revolver felt heavy in her grip as she made her way to the door. Cradled against her with her other arm and barely visible in the blanket he was wrapped in, Danny gave a burbling sigh that ended in the softest of baby snores. She risked a glance at him, her lips curving into an amazed smile.

"You're a real little mountain man, all right," she breathed. "Fight when you have to, sleep when you can. That lesson's been bringing Bird males home safely since Zebediah Bird fought the British at New Orleans, Daniel Tyler."

There was a good chance Tye had managed to arm himself, if Hawkins had told him about the vermin rifle kept in the courtyard's gardening shed, she thought, creeping through the dark kitchen. Sightlessly she fumbled on the counter for the keys she'd seen there earlier.

Her fingers closed over them. She grabbed them up just as she heard the flat crack of a shot being squeezed off, noticeably different from the more explosive sound of the guns the intruders were using. Tye had found the rifle, she thought shakily. With any luck his first shot had found a target.

He'd seen Daniel's baby monitor and he'd immediately realized she was here. She didn't know how she was so sure of that, but she was. She'd felt it— the same current that had run through her when he'd placed a newly delivered Daniel into her arms a week ago.

She hadn't imagined it then. She hadn't imagined it tonight. And what it meant she was never going to find out.

He kept saving her. She kept leaving him.

She was going to have to leave him now, and pray he and Hawkins could hold off their attackers until help arrived, she told herself. Her hand shook so badly she could hardly turn the knob on the door in front of her.

Greta's pickup truck was her workhorse, but the red four-by-four was her pride and joy—which was why she'd had a walk-through garage built for it, complete with an automatic door that opened onto the arrow-straight drive leading to the road. Susannah hastened to the vehicle.

"As soon as that garage door opens Mama's going to be puttin' the pedal to the metal, Danny Tye," she said to the sleeping baby in her arms. "Good thing your aunt Greta bought a car seat for you. She—she said she wanted to take her favorite guy out for a drive one of these days."

She couldn't let herself think of Greta right now, she told herself. She couldn't let herself think of anything or anyone but her baby. His life depended on it.

In a matter of seconds she had Daniel secured. She slid into the driver's seat, praying that the four-by-four could outrun whatever her pursuers were driving for at least as long as it took to get to Last Chance and alert the authorities.

And to tell Dr. Jennings to get ready for an emergency surgery, she thought. She forced the tears back, her lips tightening. The garage door remote in her hand, she pointed it at the windshield and activated it as she turned the key in the ignition.

The next moment pure terror shafted through her.

"This vehicle moves an inch and the brat doesn't see his first birthday. Hand over the keys if you want him to live."

For nine months she'd wondered what the face of

evil looked like, Susannah thought in icy fear. Now she knew.

Standing by the opened passenger-side door, with his sandy hair and average height he looked deceptively ordinary except for the ugly black automatic that fit so easily into his hand it seemed to be a deformed extension of it. The flat, compact barrel moved.

"D-don't hurt him, please." Her tongue felt as if it had cleaved to the roof of her mouth. The keys jingled crazily in her shaking fingers. As she dropped them into his outstretched palm she tried again, her words spilling out in a moan.

"You couldn't live with it on your conscience. Do what you want with me, but please don't hurt my little one."

"Ah don't rahtly get paid to have no conscience." His mockery of her speech was accompanied by a thin smile. He reverted to his own toneless voice. "God, it's been a long time since I heard cornpone as thick as that. Get out of the car, Ellie May, and don't even think about reaching for that gun by your feet."

Even as he spoke, the sound of a shot and then of returning fire came from the direction of the *portale*. Two more shots split the night, and on the heels of the second one Susannah heard a sound she'd never heard before.

A man was screaming. Tye's rifle had found a target. As the scream broke off abruptly and she half fell, half stumbled from the vehicle, the man beside her stiffened. Then he shrugged.

"Lucky for me I won the toss and came after you. Whoever your friend is, he's done this before, but I'm a professional, too. Kneel down on the floor and it'll all be over in a minute.''

''*Why?*'' Instead of complying, Susannah stood her ground, her desperate gaze holding his. ''Why have you people been hunting me? Why do you want to *kill* me?''

''I'll give you the same answer I gave your husband. Payback. Which reminds me—I guess I'd better take something in the way of confirmation.'' Roughly pulling her purse from her, he set it on the hood of the vehicle and carelessly tipped it upside down. Her wallet spilled out first. ''So that's why it was so hard getting a line on you. No credit cards. No ATM card. Not as dumb as we figured, are you?'' Unzipping an inner pocket, he drew out a folded paper.

''My wedding certificate,'' she said, the fear in her voice overlaid with a thread of trembling anger. ''One day Daniel's going to ask, and I want to be able to show him his daddy and me were married when we made him.''

''Since the brat's never going to get old enough to worry about it now, I'll just take this for—''

''*No!*''

Even as she lunged at him he brought his hand up and shoved her back, with no more emotion than if he was swatting a fly. His features tightening impatiently, he turned to the passenger side of the four-by-four, but by then Susannah had regained her balance, and before he'd taken more than a step she launched herself at his back and was on him.

''Not my baby! You don't even *touch* him!'' The terrified order came out in a thick, clogged voice she didn't recognize as hers. Her grasping fingers went instinctively for his face. ''You don't touch my baby!''

''What the—''

His words were a disbelieving snarl. Turning so swiftly that one of her hands almost lost its grip, he made an inarticulate sound of rage when he found she was still clinging to his back. He stumbled against the garage wall and Susannah felt the skin being abraded from her arm as it scraped along the rough concrete.

''Damn you, bitch, let go of me!'' His hands, one of them still holding the gun, wrenched at her wrists and managed to break her hold. She fell from him, striking her head against the wall as she did and landing jarringly on the floor at his feet.

''Goddammit, you could have blinded me!'' He thrust his scratched face into hers, his features twisted in rage. ''Did you think you could stop me from sending the brat along with you—''

''Over here!''

The shout came from just past the opened garage door. As the sandy-haired man's head jerked up and he instinctively swung his gun around, the very air seemed to tear apart with the force of a double explosion. Susannah saw his head snap back, saw the just-fired gun drop from his hand, saw him fall to the floor beside her. She caught one horrific glimpse of his blood-soaked chest and scrambled to her feet, instant nausea rising at the back of her throat.

She made it to the front bumper of the vehicle before she threw up.

''For God's sake, did he hurt you, Suze? Where's Danny?''

Even before the hoarsely urgent questions had left

Tyler's lips he was beside her, an arm around her hunched shoulders, a hand holding back her hair as the thin bile spilled from her. She raised her head, wiping her mouth with the back of a trembling hand. Pulling from him, she ran to the passenger side of the vehicle.

In the past fifteen minutes her baby had been taken from his bed and hastily strapped into a car, and the world had exploded around him. But there was a contented little bubble of spit at the corner of the rosebud mouth. Danny exhaled softly in his sleep, and the bubble burst.

Susannah's eyes flooded. She started to pull the edge of the blanket up around his shoulders, but her hand was shaking too badly to complete the small task.

"He's grown."

Gently moving her aside, Tye adjusted the blanket. He stood for a moment looking down at the child who'd been named for him and another strong man, and Susannah stood looking at him.

The T-shirt he was wearing was ripped at the shoulder, with a dark V-shaped patch of sweat running from the neckband to the middle of that washboard stomach. One tanned bicep sported a still-bleeding gash. Dried blood mixed with dirt smeared a hard cheekbone.

And still there was a golden glow about him.

"Babies—babies do that," she answered unevenly. "The other shooters, Tye—they could be anywhere. We should—"

"I got one. Two, I guess," he corrected himself, his jaw tensing as he flicked a glance over his shoulder at the body in the corner of the garage. "The one I took out first got hauled away by his buddy. The speed their car was going, with any luck they'll break an axle before they make it to a paved road and Sheriff Bannerman and his men will find them. The man I came here with, Del Hawkins, should have made the call by now," he added.

"And Greta? I saw her get hit, Tye," she said, her fearful gaze on his. "We're going to have to get her to—"

"She's beyond any help Doc Jennings can give her," he said, his voice harsh with emotion. "Del's getting a medical chopper out here."

Susannah closed her eyes, unbearable pain rushing through her. "I—I brought this to her," she whispered. "She took me and Danny in, and the men who are after me got her instead. I should have known they'd find me here, Tye! I had no right to put her at risk like this!"

"Listen to me!" His hands were on her shoulders. He gave her a small shake, sharp enough that her eyes flew open and she raised her gaze to his in shock. His face was grim.

"If anyone's at fault, I am. I should have pushed Bannerman harder when I realized he wasn't convinced of my story the day I found you gone. I should have guessed someone had taken you in, instead of hitting gas stations and motels asking if anyone had seen a woman with a baby who looked like she didn't belong with whoever was transporting her. But I didn't. I'll never forgive myself for that."

A muscle moved at the side of his jaw. His eyes,

bluer than heaven in the tan of his face, blazed down at her.

"And I'll never forgive myself for leaving you and Daniel unprotected," he grated. "It won't happen again. From now on I'm not letting the two of you out of my sight."

He kept saving her and she kept leaving him, Susannah thought again, meeting his gaze and experiencing again that almost-painful current flowing from him to her and back again. It seemed he'd decided to change the pattern.

For a moment she couldn't identify the feeling spreading through her. Then she recognized it for what it was. For the first time in nine months she felt completely, totally safe.

And that didn't make any sense at all.

Because something told her that looking into those blue, fallen-angel eyes was the most dangerous thing a God-fearing widow and mother could do.

Chapter Three

The grim lines bracketing Tye's mouth bore witness to the past five tension-filled hours he and Susannah had spent waiting for news of Greta. But as he replaced the receiver on the wall-mounted telephone in Del Hawkins's kitchen and turned to her, his expression held more than a touch of thankfulness.

"She's finally out of surgery. Her doctor told Del she's going to pull through."

At his announcement, sudden moisture filled Susannah's eyes. She made no effort to blink away the relieved tears as he went on, his shrug slightly dubious.

"The surgeon said she must have had a guardian angel watching over her. If the bullet hadn't been deflected by her breastbone the way it was, Greta wouldn't have stood a chance of surviving."

"Thank God," she said simply, sinking into one of the hoop-backed chairs ringing the massive table—a table, she'd learned from Tye on the drive here to Hawkins's ranch, that normally seated over a dozen rowdy male teens rather than one exhausted female with a baby, since the ranch was some kind of a boot camp for wayward youths. Despite the warm glow from the brass oil lantern hanging overhead, Danny, his carry-cot sitting in the center of the polished pine surface, was sleeping peacefully. With an unsteady finger she pushed a wisp of spun-silk hair from his forehead.

"She said she didn't believe in miracles, didn't she, little man?" she said huskily. "Guess that didn't make a speck of difference to Him. He just went ahead and gave her one."

She raised her gaze to Tye. "You let Del know we'd help his hired hands look after everything here?"

"Yeah." Rolling his shoulders as if to massage out a stiffness, Tye grimaced. "Probably Johnson and Bradley could have handled things by themselves, but I told him I still remembered how to muck out a stall, although it had been a while since he'd taught me. I'm not sure he believed me." A ghost of a smile momentarily lifted his lips. "Damn fool said he'd get home for a few hours later today to check on things. I passed on Bannerman's message about dropping by to give a formal statement, so he'll do that first, but he won't be able to tell him anything more than I could."

He didn't say what Susannah knew they were both thinking. Whatever Del could or couldn't tell the sheriff wouldn't matter, if her own interview with the lawman was anything to go by. It had been as fruitless as had all the previous interviews with the police in the past nine months—more so, in fact, since Sheriff Bannerman hadn't even wanted to hear what she had to say. He'd taken one look at the spent shells and bullet casings littering the *portale* and his expression had closed.

"A partnership gone sour, that's what I'm putting my money on. Only a drug war generates this kind of firepower," he'd declared, rubbing his jaw. "Hassell used to be a model, didn't she? They live a pretty fast life, from what I hear. Maybe her past caught up with her, or maybe those trips she's always making to New York and L.A. are about selling something other than paintings."

Beside him Tye had started to protest, and Bannerman had turned on him. "Hell, Adams, I've seen those daubs she calls art. Don't tell me people are crazy enough to shell out big money for something that doesn't even look like a real picture. I'll arrange protection for you while we're looking for the two shooters who got away, Miz Barrett, but I'll wager you weren't their primary target."

Susannah had been close enough to Tye to see the anger in his eyes as he spoke, his words measured. "Couple things, Sheriff." His tone had been ominously mild. "First and foremost, Susannah's my responsibility. That's what I do for a living, as I've told you." Before Bannerman could respond he went on. "Secondly, if she wasn't being targeted tonight why did a hit man come within seconds of taking her out, for God's sake?"

"Miz Barrett was in the wrong place at the wrong time. When she tried to run they probably thought she was trying to get away with whatever it was they'd come for." Bannerman's grunt had been dismissive. "Save the convoluted deductions for those movie detectives you rub shoulders with in Hollywood, Adams. Like I told you last week when you came to me insisting I investigate Miz Barrett's so-called abduction, things are usually a whole lot less complicated in the real world. When we get the results back on the dead man's prints I'll wager it turns out he worked for one of the big dealers.''

At that the older man had turned on a booted heel and strode off, the subject obviously closed as far as he was concerned. Tye hadn't gone after him but had helped Susannah gather up a few essentials for herself and Daniel before informing a deputy that they could be reached at the Double B if Bannerman needed them.

''If we're talking miracles you might want to send up a prayer of thanks that Del's latest crop of bad boys left a few days ago and the next batch isn't due till next month.''

Recalled to the present by his words, Susannah saw Tye had crossed to the old-fashioned sink, a battered tin coffeepot in his hand. ''Livestock I can handle. A dozen or so juvenile delinquents with chips on their shoulders would be too much for anyone to take.'' He twisted the cold-water tap and shrugged. ''Anyone but Del, that is,'' he added, his back to her.

Earlier this evening when he'd hustled her and Danny out of the garage and away from the body of the man he'd shot, he'd kept his arm protectively around her shoulders, as if he was afraid of letting her get too far away from him. Even when the helicopter Del had requested had touched down just beyond the devastated patio's walls and an unconscious Greta had been carefully lifted onto a stretcher—not by hospital paramedics, Susannah had realized numbly at the time, but by figures in military uniform—Tye had left her side only long enough to exchange a few hurried sentences with Del and an officer whom she'd seen salute Hawkins as the men had loaded their precious cargo. It wasn't until the chopper was lifting off and a wail of sirens had pierced the desert night, signalling the arrival in force of the local law, that he'd detached himself from her.

And *detached* was the right word, she thought unhappily now, taking in the straight line of his back and his precise movements as he set the coffeepot on the ancient cast-iron cook stove. She'd told Greta tonight—had it really been just a few hours ago? she wondered in tired amazement—that she'd done Tyler Adams a wrong. It was time to put that wrong right, if she could.

"Sugar-cured ham and sunny-side-up okay with you?" He threw the query over his shoulder as he opened the restaurant-size refrigerator and pulled out a bowl of brown eggs. "There's not much point in going to bed now if I'm starting chores in a few hours, so I might as well make us some breakfast. Give me a second here and I'll show you the spare first-floor bedroom. No cribs in the place as far as I know, but maybe we can rig something up with a dresser drawer for Danny to sleep in."

"I'll cook." Rising from the table, she went to a hook on the wall and took down the striped cotton teacloth she'd noticed hanging there. It was big enough to serve as an apron and deftly she wrapped it around her waist, securing it with a neat knot. As Tye set a platter holding half a huge ham on the counter, she put a restraining hand on his arm.

Beneath her fingers was solid muscle. Warmth

flooded through her before she tamped down the inappropriate reaction.

"Bannerman said you reported me missing. I—I'm sorry you were worried about us, Tye." Her hand was still resting on his arm and she let it slip to her side. "I hoped you'd just put us out of your mind and continue on your way, I guess."

This time the rush of warmth in her cheeks was shame. As her guilty gaze met his skeptical one, she shook her head.

"Oh, that's a lie, and not even a white one," she said, sliding her palms against the tea towel. "Granny Lacey used to say Mr. Scratch started with a body's tongue first when he was trying to take over, and she was right. I knew you'd probably be looking for us, but when Greta showed up the way she did all I could think of was keeping Danny safe. It was like the story of baby Moses in the rush basket floating downstream out of danger," she ended inadequately.

"Sorry, honey." Under the once-white and now begrimed T-shirt he wore, broad shoulders lifted in a controlled shrug. "I'm far from being the Bible scholar you seem to be, so you lost me at the end there. But I'll accept what you said about lying just now. You didn't hope I'd forgotten you, Suze. You knew damn well I wouldn't, just like I knew damn well you weren't about to forget me anytime soon. Who the hell's Mr. Scratch?"

"You swear too much." Even as the automatic comment left her lips Susannah knew it was more of a defense than a reproof. Was it was her imagination or had the space between them, slight as it had been in the first place, lessened somehow? She took a step away from him, all her earlier misgivings suddenly flooding back.

Could you call a man beautiful? she asked herself, forcing a deep breath into her lungs in an attempt to dispel the unfamiliar edginess that was electrifying all her nerve endings. But breathing was a mistake. As she inhaled, the very scent of him seemed to rush into her—a scent compounded of cordite and skin salt and the faintest trace of the soap he'd presumably used earlier this evening.

He *was* beautiful. He was beautiful the way a stallion was beautiful, beautiful the way a timber wolf standing over its prey could be beautiful, beautiful because he was a perfectly built male animal.

And that overpowering maleness could make even someone like her forget everything else except the basic fact that she was a female.

"Mr. Scratch is the devil," she said, making herself turn back to face him. "Bible scholar or not, you must have heard of him."

"Red tail and horns, pointed beard?" He hacked off a couple of slices of ham, his question disinterested, and something about the careless tone of his voice roused a tiny spark of anger in her.

"I don't think that's what he looks like at all," she said. "If he did we'd be able to recognize him, and he couldn't do us any harm. If you'll show me where Del keeps his skillets I'll take over from here, Tye. I'm not partial to having a man in the way when I'm cooking."

She started to move past him toward the stove, her posture rigid, but even as she took a second step he was in front of her, barring her way.

"Okay, so tell me, Suze," he said, his tone edged. "How do you know him when you see him? What exactly does he look like, your Mr. Scratch?"

His hands were on her shoulders, and suddenly the worn cotton of her dress felt as insubstantial as shattered silk. He tightened his grip by a fraction, and at the barely noticeable adjustment she felt the fabric of her bodice tautening against the swell of her breasts. Instant heat suffused her, and this time when she tried to breathe she found she couldn't. She stared up at him, her gaze painfully wide.

Steal the blue from the most perfect summer sky on the most perfect summer's day and you'd have his eyes, she told herself. A woman could fall into that blue—fall straight in and never want to come out again. What would it be like to let those eyes see every inch of you, to feel that mouth everywhere on your skin, to forget everything you'd ever been taught and give yourself for just one sinful night to the de—

The breath she'd been trying to take slammed into her with the force of an arctic gale, sweeping away all heat and replacing the lassitude that had gripped her with cold awareness. She swallowed past the dryness in her throat, and he released his grip on her.

"I—I think he looks just like you, Tye," she said unevenly. "That's why he's so dangerous."

Just for a moment she would have sworn she saw something flash behind those eyes—something that could have been pain. Before she could identify the emotion it was gone.

Or maybe it hadn't been there in the first place. A crooked smile lifted a corner of his mouth.

"What's that expression about giving a dog a bad

name?'' This time it wasn't her imagination. Without seeming to move at all, suddenly he'd lessened the distance between them to no more than a few inches. Behind her she felt the hard edge of the counter pressing into her back.

''Give a dog a bad name and he'll bite?'' she ventured. ''Tye, I—''

''That's it.'' He bent his head, obliterating the last of her precious buffer zone. ''You can call me off anytime, Suze,'' he said, his tone velvety. ''But maybe you don't want to. Maybe after a lifetime of putting the devil behind you, just this once you'd like to be tempted.''

His last words were murmured against her lips. For the space of a heartbeat his gaze held hers, and during that heartbeat Susannah knew she should step away from him.

Her lips parted. Her veins felt suddenly as if they were filled with something much thicker than blood, something so heavy and hot she found it impossible to move her limbs. An identical heat pooled in the pit of her stomach and seemed to spill downward toward her thighs.

She heard herself sigh, the sound so light and insubstantial it was barely audible. His mouth came down onto hers before the soft exhalation was completed.

Tye's tongue moved past her lips, past her teeth, and without conscious volition she felt herself opening up to him, her startled reaction based on instinct rather than experience. The next moment his palms were on either side of her face, pulling her closer to him and steadying her. His tongue went a little deeper, as if it were trying to coax her very soul from her, and some last spark of self-preservation flared desperately inside her.

With the half-formed intention of pushing him away she brought her hands up, but even as her fingers spread against the solidity of his chest he lifted his head.

"You don't have to do that. I said you could call me off anytime." His whisper was hoarse, his breath warm on her lips. "But you don't trust the devil, do you? Is that why you ran from me the day you disappeared, Suze—because you were afraid of what I was?"

Dazedly she shook her head, her gaze locked on his. "I don't think so." The heat that had been spreading through her was now a searing ache. Her throat felt scratchy and raw as she forced the words out. "I don't think that was it at all. I think I ran because I was afraid of what *I* was, Tye. Or of what I wanted to be, from the first moment I saw you," she ended, her voice low.

His gaze darkened to indigo. "I don't get it. What did you want to be?"

She didn't reply immediately. Instead she allowed herself to drink in the sight of him, needing every detail her gaze lingered on to be imprinted in her mind—the tanned cheekbones, the thick and incongruously dark lashes half veiling his eyes, the chiselled cut of his mouth. A muscle moved at the side of his jaw. She attempted a smile, and knew her attempt had failed.

"Why, everything I wasn't, of course," she said

softly. "Beautiful and sophisticated and—and sexy, the kind of woman a man like you would be used to."

She stepped away from him, staring down at the tea towel around her waist. She blinked, and tightened the loosened knot. Although this time her lips curved as she wanted them to, she felt a stinging moisture behind her eyes.

"When I looked at you I didn't want to be me. And I knew that was wrong."

Susannah glanced toward the table, where Danny was still fast asleep in his carry-cot. She took a deep breath. "He's my world, Tye. I can't let anything get in the way of keeping him safe, and no matter what Sheriff Bannerman thinks, those men showed up tonight looking to find me. So even if you're right and I knew I wasn't going to forget you when Greta stopped to help me that day, I couldn't let myself think about that. I still can't."

Tye held her gaze for a second longer. Then he looked away, his shoulders lifting again in that half shrug she'd seen him give before, as if he were unconsciously trying to adjust the weight of a burden he couldn't rid himself of. When he spoke there was a harsh edge to his voice.

"Want to hear something funny, Suze? When I looked at you I didn't want to be me, either. And just for a while I persuaded myself there was a chance I could change."

He exhaled tightly. "Bannerman might have taken your disappearance more seriously if anyone but me had reported it. I should have known I couldn't wipe the past out by coming back here. Like Greta, I've never believed in miracles, so I don't know why I let myself hope I'd been handed one.''

"I don't understand," she said, troubled by the bleakness in his words. A moment ago the man in front of her had been holding her so closely she'd been afraid she was in danger of losing herself in him. Now he seemed once again to be separated from her by an insurmountable wall—a wall not only isolating him from her, but from everything else around him. He turned to face her, his smile humorless.

"You don't have to understand. All you have to know is that what just happened between us was a one-time only thing. For what it's worth, you've got my word I won't cross the line again." He scrubbed his jaw with a weary hand. "I think it's time you filled me in on the details. Do you have any idea who those men were or what they wanted from you?"

His change of subject was briskly abrupt, but probably that was for the best, she thought. Out of some sense of responsibility for her and the baby he'd helped deliver, Tye Adams had appointed himself her temporary protector, but that was as far as their relationship could go. From the start she'd known they came from two different worlds and although some part of her had fleetingly yearned to fit into his, she was too much Lacey Bird's granddaughter ever to attempt to be something she wasn't.

She had no idea why he'd kissed her. She frowned at the platter of ham and reached for the carving knife beside it before answering his question.

"I've never known who they are. As for what they want, the man who tried to kill me tonight said it was payback." Carefully she concentrated on evening up the hacked surface of the meat and cutting two perfect slices. "After he was killed the police told me Frank hadn't been a photojournalist like he'd always said, but a gambler and a small-time scam artist whose real name was probably Jerry Corning—although he'd used so many different aliases over the years they weren't even sure of that. I guess one of his scams backfired on him in the end. Obviously not all of his marks were as gullible as I was."

On her last sentence her voice wavered and to her chagrin the knife slipped in her hand, almost nicking her. Immediately Tye took the implement.

"Forget the damned cooking, I'll rustle us up something." Briskly he opened one of the lower cupboards and pulled out a cast-iron frypan. "I did KP duty here in my day, and while I never was the cook Jess or Connor was, I was a hell of a lot better than Riggs."

He shot her a glance. "That's right, honey. I was one of Del's hell-raisers when I was a teen. I think that might have had something to do with Bannerman's attitude tonight, since during our year at the ranch the four of us weren't exactly popular with him."

The man was impossible to read, Susannah thought helplessly. He had the good looks of a movie star, but from what he'd said he'd built up a business providing physical security for celebrities instead of becoming one himself. The privileged aura he unconsciously projected could only have come from a background of money and power so well entrenched he'd grown up taking it for granted, and yet apparently he'd come close to throwing it all away when he'd been younger.

Earlier tonight he'd been put into the position of

having to kill a killer. If he felt any regret for taking a life, whatever the circumstances, he'd given no sign. But just now he'd brought up the subject of his past for the sole reason, she suspected, of distracting her from her own unhappy memories.

She smiled shakily at him. "I think my sympathies are with Sheriff Bannerman. You and your bad-boy friends must have torn up the county. No, Tye—" Firmly she took the pan from him. "I'd rather have something to do while I'm telling you my story, and kitchen work's always been more of a comfort than a chore for me. Besides, that ham needs red-eye gravy, and I'll bet a dollar a Californian like you doesn't know the first thing about making it."

"You'd win that dollar." A corner of his mouth lifted. "All right, Suze, you get to cook. Do you trust me to get Dan the Man into something a little more like a real bed?"

"Dan the—" A few minutes ago she hadn't imagined she would be capable of laughing, but the sound bubbling up from her throat definitely was a laugh, Susannah realized. And although she'd even had foolish, first-mama nerves when Greta had asked once or twice if she could put Danny to bed, for some reason she had no qualms about Tye's competence in tucking her baby in. Well, almost no qualms, she admitted.

"Line the dresser drawer with something padded," she said as he lifted the carry-cot and its tiny occupant from the table. "And Tye—he likes his blanket up to his chest, no farther. But don't cover his hands, because then he'll wake up for sure and start fretting—"

"Wonder where he gets that from?" His question was accompanied by the slightest of smiles. "Hey, lady—don't forget I was the first one to hold the little guy. As I recall, I didn't give you any static when you asked me to hand him over for a while.''

''That's true.'' A second soft bubble of laughter rose up in her. With exaggerated deliberation, she turned away, reaching for the bowl of eggs as she slid the pan on the burner.

''Suze?''

At the unexpectedly tentative note in his voice her pose of unconcern fled. Glancing quickly at him, she saw that he'd paused in the doorway. His gaze met hers, the humor that had lit his eyes only a moment ago no longer in evidence.

''Were you very much in love with him?'' he asked softly. Even as the words left his lips he frowned impatiently. ''Sorry, stupid question. Of course you were—the man was your husband, for God's sake.'' He turned toward the hall, but before he could take a second step, Susannah spoke, her own tone as low as his had been.

''Yes, Frank Barrett was my husband. And twelve hours after I became his wife I was a widow.''

Blindly she extracted an egg from the bowl, finding its cool, spherical surface somehow comforting.

''He was killed the morning after our wedding night, while I was out walking along the beach wondering if there was any way I could undo the mistake I'd made in marrying him.''

Chapter Four

"For a while after Granny Lacey died I felt like I'd been cast adrift. She'd been my anchor all my life, and suddenly she was gone. I think Frank sensed that."

Neatly, Susannah laid her knife and fork at the edge of her plate and pressed a corner of the red-and-white checked napkin to her lips. Across the table from her Tye took a last mouthful of ham. "More coffee?" she asked, half rising from her chair.

But already he was up, and waving her back into her seat. "I'll get it. Did the police ever catch the hit-and-run driver who killed her?"

"No."

Falling silent as he hefted the blue-enamelled coffeepot from the stove, she allowed herself to watch him through her lashes. For all his height and breadth there was an easy grace to the most casual of his movements, but it was a controlled grace, as if on some level he held himself ready to react instantaneously to any given situation. He'd changed out of the begrimed T-shirt into a faded chambray shirt. The garment was obviously work attire, Susannah conceded, but even coming upon him dressed the way he was and pumping gas at a service station there was no way anyone would mistake Tyler Adams for hired labor.

It wasn't the first time since Frank's death she'd had to relate the facts of her brief marriage and sudden widowhood, and she'd grown to dread the shocked sympathy and carefully phrased condolences that invariably resulted. She hadn't wanted that from Tye— hadn't wanted, even for a moment, to mislead him as to how it had really been. After telling him what she'd never told anyone else she'd looked down at the egg in her hand, half surprised to see it was still intact. His response had been immediate.

"The guilt's been the hardest to bear, right?" he'd said shortly. "Been there, done that, Suze. Let's put this talk off until you get some hot coffee and food inside you. All things considered it's been a crappy night all around for you and the way I acted a while ago was part of that, I'm sure."

He'd understood up to a point, she thought now. But that point had stopped short of realizing that for the few moments he'd held her in his arms the rest of what had happened tonight had faded from her consciousness. He certainly couldn't suspect that if he'd held her for a single second longer, Frank Barrett's widow and little Daniel Tyler's mother might not only have given in to temptation, as he'd suggested, but would have done her level best to tempt *him.*

Which would have been about as out of place as a mule trying to outpace Dan Patch, she chastised herself mentally. *Thank the Lord you didn't totally forget yourself with the man.*

"Did the authorities say anything that made you

think they suspected—'' Stopping in midsentence, Tye refilled her coffee cup and then his before he sat down. He caught her inquiring glance and shook his head dismissively. "I'm jumping the gun here. You said your grandmother had been your anchor. What happened to your parents?"

"By the time I was five they were both dead," she said simply. "Granny Lacey never liked to talk about it much, and about all she'd ever say was that my mama might have lived if she'd had a stronger heart, but that she never would have been the same after. My grandmother's sister died of a fever, so I guess having her daughter-in-law go the same way hit her hard."

She took a sip of her coffee. "Hit my daddy hard, too, from all accounts," she added softly. "I don't remember much about that time, but I recall the last time I saw him. I think it must have been a few months after Mama passed away, because Granny Lacey was living with us and looking after me. Daddy came into my bedroom to hear me say my prayers, and he asked me to say one specially for him. I felt his hand on my head just as I was finishing, but by the time I got off my knees and hopped into bed he'd gone. He was killed in a car accident that night, and within a week Granny Lacey had packed up everything we owned and she and I left Fox Hollow for good."

"Tough for her, with a granddaughter to care for and raise all by herself," Tye commented. Susannah looked up in surprise.

"She never felt she was carrying the burden alone—just like I know I'm not raising Danny all by myself." She saw belated comprehension touch his features, followed almost immediately by discomfort, and she shot him a mischievous smile. "Don't worry, I won't start leaving religious tracts around for you to read, Tye. But even though I haven't been back for sixteen years I'll always be a Fox Hollow girl, and folks in Fox Hollow are pretty rock solid in the Word."

"I don't believe in much of anything," he said dryly. "But we're straying from the subject. Lacey Bird took her granddaughter and moved to New Jersey, of all places? That jalopy you were driving had Garden State plates," he added.

"Goodness, that wasn't the first place we lived after pulling up stakes." Frowning, Susannah spread out the fingers of one hand and started ticking them off. "I started school in Ohio, I remember, and I got to grade four before Granny Lacey was asked by a women's center in Indiana to give midwifery training there. For a time she worked with a group of Amish midwives in Pennsylvania and then I think we moved to upper New York—no—" she corrected herself thoughtfully "—we stayed in Kentucky that summer. I was old enough to take a part-time job at the Dairy Queen and start helping with the money. We never had much but we always got by."

"On delivering babies." There was a slightly skeptical note in his voice. She didn't take offense.

"On delivering babies, on taking in sewing, on the waitressing jobs I got when I finished my schooling," she agreed. "I made good grades but I wasn't scholarship material so college wasn't an option, and although Granny said we could manage some kind of training for me if I wanted, I liked working in restaurants. I liked it that people came in hungry and left full. Does that sound foolish?''

"No." A corner of Tye's mouth quirked upward. "But it's a different attitude from the one I'm used to hearing. Most of my clients are on a permanent diet. Why did you end up in New Jersey?''

"Granny Lacey felt she'd been called to go there." On the heels of his diet remark as it was, her answer came out more snappishly than she'd intended. She went on less briskly. "Five months after we moved to Atlantic City she was walking home one night from the bus stop after delivering a baby. A car mounted the curb and struck her, killing her instantly. I still hadn't really gotten over her death when Frank started coming into the diner where I worked and asking me out.''

Tye seemed to pick his next words with care. "From what you said earlier I get the impression it wasn't love at first sight on your part, Suze.''

"So why did I go out with him, you mean?'' She looked down at her hands. "I was lonely. And Frank made me laugh.''

She glanced swiftly up at him, but his face was impassive. "I'd been on church outings with groups and there'd been a pastor's son who'd accompanied me to an organ recital once, but I'd never really dated before. Heavens, it wasn't until I was nineteen that I bought my first lip gloss, and although she didn't say anything I could tell Granny Lacey considered it pretty racy on my part. I guess what I'm trying to say is that I had an old-fashioned upbringing. I'm not sorry I did, but maybe it didn't equip me that well when I suddenly found myself on my own. He was in his thirties and good-looking. I—I was flattered by his interest in me.''

''And he told you he was what—a photojournalist? You believed him?'' The note of skepticism was back in his voice. This time it stung.

''He said he was a freelancer travelling around looking for interesting stories, which explained why he lived out of motels instead of having a permanent place of his own. Yes, I believed him. Since the police later told me he was a con man, I figure I wasn't the first person to have been taken in by Frank Barrett or Jerry Corning or whatever his name originally was. That doesn't make me stupid, Tye.''

She took a deep breath. ''I found out he'd lied to me about a lot of things, but in his own way Frank cared for me—cared enough to ask me to marry him. He said he wanted a family, and I wanted that, too. So I accepted his proposal, and I married him, and if anyone cheated anyone I was the one who cheated him. Deep down he wasn't a bad man, Tye. He deserved better from his wife.''

''You said the morning after your wedding night you left him sleeping and went for a walk along the beach.'' Across the table from her, he leaned back in his chair and folded his arms over his chest. ''When you got back to the hotel what had you decided to tell him?''

Susannah blinked. ''Why, nothing, of course. What could I say—that I'd changed my mind? We'd exchanged vows. I was a married woman. The only right thing for me to do was to make the best marriage I could with...'' Her words trailed off. Her gaze searched his face. "I can't let myself off that lightly, Tye. Yes, I would have stayed with him if he'd lived. But marriage is supposed to be more than just a contract."

"Is it?" As if prompted by a sudden restlessness, abruptly he pushed his chair back and stood. "As far as I'm concerned, that's all it is. I should know, since I grew up with Marvin Adams for a father."

He shrugged down at her. "Believe me, if you were a Hollywood spouse you would have heard of him. Hell, you'd probably have his card tucked safely away somewhere just in case you ever needed it. Greatest divorce attorney in California, bar none, and when the matrimonial home, the ski lodge in Aspen, and the residuals from the television series are put on the chopping block to be divided, no one ever says anything about fifty percent of the love, honey."

He exhaled impatiently. "But hey, that's just my take on it. Let's get back to your story—you returned to the hotel that morning and found someone had whacked your new husband, right?"

His tone was as harsh as his phrasing, and shocked, Susannah stared at him. "Sounds to me like you've got issues with your daddy, Tye," she said evenly. "That's no reason to make light of murder. My husband's life was taken. The baby we'd made the night before never had a chance to know his father. I got back to the hotel and found someone had shot Frank through the heart while he was still lying in our marriage bed."

She got stiffly to her feet. Needing something to do with her shaking hands, she gathered up their plates and walked by him to the sink. "The police were already there. After I identified Frank's body they took me down to the precinct and asked me if I knew anyone who held a grudge against him or if he had any enemies, but of course I couldn't tell them much and I got the feeling they were just going through the motions anyway. It was only at his funeral a few days later I found out why. One of the detectives assigned to the case met me as I was leaving the cemetery and told me he thought I should know what they'd discovered about Frank—that he wasn't what he'd said he was, wasn't even *who* he'd said he was. He'd been in prison up until a month before I'd met him, serving a sentence for fraud.''

Carefully she stacked the plates in the sink. She turned to him. ''I could remember that about Danny Tye's daddy and talk about him getting whacked. Or I could remember the kindnesses he showed me, the fact that he arranged to have a preacher marry us because he knew how much it meant to me, the way he sometimes looked at me when he spoke about having a family of our own someday. I think he wanted to be the man he told me he was. I think if he'd lived he might have become that man. But someone took that away from him, Tye. Someone murdered him. And then they came after me.''

She'd thought of him as an angel, albeit a fallen one, Susannah thought unhappily. She'd wondered at one point if he was the devil. If she was just now finding out that Tye Adams was a mere mortal it was her own fault. He dealt with violence on a daily basis. It had to have hardened him.

''Where does Del keep his dish soap?'' she asked, attempting to even out the emotion in her tone.

"Might as well wash these before my little mister wakes up and starts fretting for his first meal of the—"

"You're disappointed in me. I'm disappointed in myself." Even as he spoke Tye's hands were on her shoulders, gently turning her from the sink to face him. A muscle moved in his jaw. "The latter's nothing new, but for some reason I'm finding the first one harder to take than I would have thought. You're right, Suze—a man's life was snuffed out, and brutally. I apologize for the way I spoke."

"It wasn't just one man's life."

She could either look into his face or straight ahead at the solid wall of his chest. But the top two buttons of the chambray shirt were unfastened, revealing a smooth golden-tan slice of skin only inches from her, and at the sight of that smooth skin, all at once she had an overwhelming and totally unprecedented impulse to lean forward and touch the tip of her tongue to it. Susannah's face flamed as she jerked her gaze upward. She went on hurriedly, wanting—no, *needing*—to put some space between them as soon as she could.

"A few weeks later the owner of the diner where I worked was helping me take the garbage to the bins in the alleyway behind the building."

The out-of-place heat that had momentarily flared in her died as the memory replayed itself in her mind. "Mr. Stephanopoulos had been so good to me, contributing toward the costs of the funeral, going to the police station with me to check on the progress of the investigation, giving me time off with pay. He—he was the first person I told when I found out I was pregnant with Danny," she said softly. "He said a baby was always cause for celebration, no matter what the circumstances."

"What happened in the alleyway?" Tye's prompting was gentle. The darkness in his eyes told Susannah he knew what she was about to say.

"A car slowed down on the street. I didn't think anything of it—sometimes people thought there might be parking round back, and they drove by slowly checking for a space. The next minute I heard gunfire and saw flashes coming from the car before it sped off, and when I looked over at Mr. Stephanopoulos he was holding his chest. He was dead before he fell, Tye."

For nine long months she'd tried to stay strong for the baby growing inside her. Fear had been a luxury she couldn't afford, any more than she could afford the luxury of breaking down in tears whenever the tension and the memories got to be too much. Bird stock was tough stock, Granny Lacey had often said— not always law-abiding stock, not always with the most book-learning, but tough enough to take what life threw at it and survive.

I have survived and I did stay strong, Susannah told herself as the lump in her throat swelled to almost painful proportions. *I'm going to have to continue being strong, because this isn't over yet. But aside from Frank and Mr. Stephanopoulos, tonight they cut down Greta and nearly got my son, so just for a few minutes I believe I'm going to let myself…let myself—*

"Go ahead and cry, Suze." His hands slid from her shoulders to her neck, and then framed her face. Although there was no humor in them the corners of his mouth softened. "The shirt's old, and salt washes out. Go ahead and cry, and then we'll figure out what we're going to do."

"But Tye, what do they *want* with me? Why did they follow me here to the one place I thought I'd be safe?"

She saw his gaze darken with confusion, but before she could elaborate she felt the first tears spill, fat and hot, over her bottom lashes. She opened her mouth to explain, but just then the lump in her throat burst and the pain came rushing out as he pulled her to his chest.

"There was so much blood—so much *blood.* It was all over the white sheets and all I could think of was that the hotel laundry was just never going to get it out. Isn't that terrible? My husband was lying there dead, and I was wondering if cold water would do the trick. Whatever he'd done, he didn't deserve what happened to him—no more than Mr. Stephanopoulos deserved to die in a filthy alleyway, no more than Greta should have been punished for taking me in. I don't know who they are or what they want, but they must be monsters, Tye, pure *evil.*"

Her words were a whispered gasp against his wet shirt. "That's what I felt by the side of the highway after you'd left to get help. I even thought I saw him— saw him out of the corner of my eye, as if a mirage was trying to take shape. The sun was turning everything into mirrors and reflections and it was getting hotter and hotter...and I thought I saw the sand coming together in the desert. I knew it was pure evil and I knew it wanted me and my baby. Then Greta drove up. When I looked again it had disappeared."

His hold around her had tightened. Now, with infinite care he gently uncurled her clenched fists from his shirt and held her just far enough away from him that he could look into her face. His features seemed carved.

"You didn't tell me this before."

She shook her head. "Because afterward when I thought about it I told myself I'd probably imagined the whole thing. But I can't completely shake the feeling that just for those few minutes the same evil that had left its mark in the hotel room where my husband was killed was closer to me and Danny than it had ever been."

She took a long, shuddering breath. Bringing the heels of her hands to her face, she smeared aside the tears that were obscuring her vision and met his gaze. Her own slowly widened as she took in his expression.

"This means something to you, doesn't it, Tye? I thought you'd tell me it couldn't have been for real— but you know what it was I saw, don't you? You don't think I imagined it at all."

"I told you I don't believe in much of anything, Suze." His tone was rough, his jaw tight. "I certainly don't believe in the Skinwalk—"

Abruptly he broke off, his whole body tensing. The next moment he'd thrust her from him and was striding toward the door. "Someone's arrived," he said sharply. "Johnson and Bradley have been taking turns camping out by the main gate these past few nights, so either one of them let someone through or—"

He didn't finish his sentence, but instead reached above the lintel and took down a heavy, old-fashioned key. He inserted it into the lock of a narrow cabinet she hadn't noticed before, built into the wall beside the door. Swinging open the door and reaching in, he withdrew a pump-action shotgun, its blued-steel barrel gleaming as if it had recently been oiled.

"It's probably nothing," he said tightly, pulling out a box of shells and one-handedly opening it. He scooped up a handful and spilled five out onto the counter before inserting the one he was still holding into the weapon's magazine. He reached for a second shell and glanced over at her. "And it might not necessarily be our friends from Greta's, come back for another try at you, Susannah. The Double B's had troubles of its own these past few weeks, which is why Del asked me here in the first place. I'll fill you in on the details later, but right now I think it's best if you stay in the bedroom with Danny while I—"

"Hand me out the Winchester that was behind the shotgun, Tye, and that box of thirty-ought-six rifle ammo I can see on the shelf above it."

He was chambering the sixth and final shell into his own weapon, Susannah saw. Without waiting for him to comply with her request she reached past him, grasping the gun and the box of cartridges. He shot her a disbelieving look.

"Put that down, Suze. I can't be worrying about you fooling around with a loaded weapon while I'm checking this situation—"

"Then don't worry." Efficiently she began loading the rifle, glancing up at him in time to see his startled frown. "Most of the places I grew up in were rural areas," she said briefly. "Granny Lacey was a country woman, too, and she didn't hold with women not knowing which end of a gun the bullet came out of."

Her task finished, she faced him. "I'll stay on the

porch, Tye,'' she said, her tone brooking no argument. ''But a few minutes ago I was crying like a little pig- tailed girl afraid of the dark, and somehow that doesn't sit real well with me. I'm a mama with a baby to protect, and since running hasn't worked I figure it's time to turn and take a stand.''

Slowly he nodded, his eyes on hers. ''Point taken. But if I see Kevin Bradley or Paul Johnson, I'm going to send them along to keep you company. I'm damn glad now I introduced you to them when we arrived, so you'll recognize them.'' He turned to the door lead- ing onto the porch, and then hesitated. ''You're cer- tain you know how to handle that thing?''

''Likely better'n you, California boy,'' she said, forcing a shaky smile to her lips. ''Tye—be careful.''

''You, too.'' His voice was husky with tension and under the denim-blue shirt his shoulders were stiff. His answering smile didn't reach his eyes. ''You, too, Suze,'' he repeated quietly as he pushed open the screen door and stepped out onto the wide verandah, Susannah close behind.

Whenever she afterward thought about the five minutes that followed, in her memory they stretched out like thirty, and thirty agonizingly slow-moving minutes at that. The ranch gate was a good half mile away from the main house and the barns, and the sound that had alerted him, Tye had told her in an undertone just before he melted into the darkened yard, had been the sudden barking, just as suddenly silenced, of Shep, Del's heeler hound that usually ac- companied Johnson or Bradley on their recently insti- gated night-time vigils. Rifle at the ready and her heart in her mouth, Susannah kept to the most shadowed

area of the porch, waiting either for some sign that
Shep's alarm had been a false one or for—

*—for the moment when I have to make the decision
whether to blow a man to kingdom come or not,* she
thought, swallowing dryly. *If it comes to that, Lord, I
pray I make the right choice, and if the right choice
means I take the shot to keep my baby from harm, I
pray You give me a steady trigger finger and good
aim.*

She wished she knew what Tye had meant when
he'd said the Double B had been experiencing its own
troubles, she thought worriedly. But whatever those
troubles were, Del had deemed them serious enough
to have his hired hands stand guard and Tye himself
had taken a weapon to confront the intruder. If this
had nothing to do with those who had been hunting
her, it still was a situation that called for an armed
response.

Even as the thought went through her mind a muf-
fled sound seemed to come from the direction of the
horse barn a few hundred feet away. She whirled to
face the bulky silhouette of the outbuilding where
Del's beloved Appaloosas, as Tye had informed her,
were stabled.

"Susannah!"

Headlights crested the rise in the drive leading to
the ranch's perimeter, and Tye's shout, coming as it
did from the open utility vehicle and holding no note
of warning, sent a rush of relief flooding through her.
Temporarily blinded by the vehicle's beams, Susannah
shielded her eyes with one hand just in time to see
him alight from it as it came to a stop.

The two other occupants in the utility got out as

Tye strode across the yard toward her, his grin illuminated by the headlights. One she recognized as Johnson, but the driver, a scruffily dressed man of medium height now hoisting a duffel bag from the back seat, was unfamiliar to her.

"False alarm," Tye said as he mounted the steps to the porch.

Taking her rifle from her, carefully he broke it open and extracted the ammunition before snapping the stock back in place and setting the unloaded weapon by the door with his own.

"I met up with Johnson on my way to the boundary fence," he went on, nodding at the taller and gaunter of the two men. "We got there just as Bradley was about to give this no-good bum his walking papers and it took all my powers of persuasion to convince him that our after-hours visitor was who he said he was. Susannah, I'd like you to meet Jess Crawford— another Double B bad boy and, despite his disreputable appearance right now, the only one of Del's former delinquents who's achieved millionaire status by purely legitimate means."

"Don't listen to him, Susannah." Dropping the duffel bag at his feet, the man Tye had just introduced took a step forward, his pleasant features breaking into a smile. "Even when we were teenagers he tried to slander me with the girls just so he'd have a fighting chance. I apologize for my late arrival and the way I look, but I've been driving all night to—"

"Adams—look!"

The urgent exclamation came from Paul Johnson. A few feet from the utility vehicle, he was standing stock-still, and something about the rigidity of his frame sent Susannah's nerve-endings on the alert. His next words confirmed her fears.

"The horse barn! It's on *fire!*"

Chapter Five

"Danny!" Susannah spun fearfully around, her hand already reaching for the handle of the screen door, but before she could yank it open Tye was gripping her shoulder.

"Wait with Danny in Jess's utility. If the blaze looks like it's going to get away from us, drive off and don't stop until you get to town. Understood?"

She nodded, her fingers tightening almost painfully on the door handle. "I understand. But Tye—I think someone started the fire. Whoever he is, I think he's still in the barn."

"An arsonist?" Behind Tye, Jess looked grim. "If this is the kind of thing Del was talking about, it seems I showed up just in time. I'll go around back and switch on the reservoir pump."

"Good man." Tye's smile flashed briefly white in the shadows. "While you and Johnson are dragging the hose over I'll start getting the horses to safety. Suze, remember what I said—don't worry about us, just make sure Dan the Man's safe. Go on, honey."

As she sped through the door he was holding open for her Susannah caught the quick appraising glance

Jess threw in her direction. Their eyes met and he gave her a comprehending grin before turning away.

She raced through the kitchen to the spare bedroom, her anxiety overlaid with confusion. It was obvious that Tye's old friend had taken Tye's casual endearment to her for something much more meaningful, but although his mistake was harmless, it would be dangerous for her to make the same erroneous assumption.

"The man's got a silver tongue, starshine, so him calling me honey all the time doesn't mean anything," she breathed as she gently lifted a yawning Danny from his makeshift crib. His fingers bunching into tiny fists, sleepily he knuckled at his eyes. She felt her breast swell with a rush of love so strong tears pricked at the back of her eyes. To cover her emotion she fixed a mock-stern look on her small son as she hastened from the room.

"I won't have you turning out the same way, young man," she remonstrated. "You're going to be a natural-born heartbreaker as it is. I'll have to teach you not to take a leaf from your namesake's book and be so free and easy when you're talking to gullible females like your mama—"

Her nervous flow of words dried up as she pushed open the screen door and stepped once more onto the porch. In scant seconds everything had changed.

The wisps of smoke that had caught Johnson's attention were now thick and greasy billows of gray pouring from the open barn doors, backlit with ruddy tongues of flame, and the screams of terrified horses added to the nightmarish quality of the scene. Even as she hesitated, Susannah saw Tye emerge from the

inferno, fighting to hold on to the bridles of two plung-
ing mares.

As soon as he was clear of the barn doors he released his grip on the fear-maddened Appaloosas. One
immediately wheeled and tried to return to the barn,
but Tye seemed to have been expecting something of
the sort and he herded the mare off into the yard before turning back to the stables.

"Miz Barrett!"

It was Johnson, his back bowed under the weight
of the heavy woven-cord hose he was hauling around
the side of the house. A little behind him Susannah
saw Jess Crawford hastily affixing a coupler between
the hose and a portable pump.

"Miz Barrett, you heard the man. You get that little
tyke into the vehicle now, hear? A fire's like a scalded
cat—you never know which way it'll jump." Despite
his admonishing words, his tone wasn't unfriendly and
his gaunt features showed only concern. Susannah
nodded.

"I'm gettin', Mr. Johnson," she said swiftly. "You
be careful, too."

Their hurried exchange galvanized her into action.
Leaving the porch she ran across the yard to the utility, Danny clasped closely to her. Only when she actually opened the vehicle's passenger door did she realize she had a problem, and a significant one.

When she and Tye had left Greta's earlier he'd
transferred Danny's infant seat from the red four-by-
four to Del's extended-size truck—the truck that was
parked, Susannah saw with a sinking heart, only feet
from the side of the horse barn.

"If we have to leave in a hurry I can't risk driving

off with you not secured, little one,'' she murmured to Danny. ''I *won't* risk it. I'm going to have to get that infant seat. You wait here for your mama, little man.''

She didn't want to leave him, she thought worriedly as she laid Danny on the wide back seat of the utility, but it was the only option she had. When they'd arrived at the ranch two hours ago, she'd seen Tye carelessly pocket the keys of Del's truck as he'd helped her transfer Danny into his carry-cot before entering the house, and since now wasn't a good time to tap him on the shoulder and ask him to hand them over to her, taking the bigger vehicle was out of the question. But he hadn't locked the truck's doors, she was sure, which meant she should be able to remove the infant seat easily enough and get it to the vehicle that was available to her.

Hastening across the yard, in the light from the now-blazing fire she saw Kevin Bradley, the Double B's other hired hand, exiting the barn with a rearing gelding. Obviously the fire had been visible to him where he'd been standing guard at the ranch's perimeter and he'd left his post to help out in the emergency. The animal's hooves flashed down perilously near Bradley's head, and with a shouted oath he released his grip. Suddenly unconstrained, the Appaloosa pounded by only yards from her and disappeared into the darkness.

''Susannah!'' Jess, his face streaked with soot, was beside her. He cast a quick glance over his shoulder to where Johnson was aiming the now-operational hose into the building, and then turned his attention back to her. "What are you doing here? Where's your son?"

"I need to get the infant seat from Del's truck," she said, and knew from his uncomprehending frown that he hadn't heard her over the mingled tumult of the fire and the horses. She tried again. "Del's truck," she shouted. "Danny's car seat—"

The rest of her sentence was obliterated by a sound even more terrible than the equine terror that had been filling her ears for the past few minutes. It was the sound of a human being in unimaginable agony, and at it, the blood in Susannah's veins seemed to turn to ice.

"Jess—*where's Tye?*"

Even as she rasped the urgent question past numb lips she saw him coming again from the barn, leading a frightened mare and a stumbling foal to safety. As he did, the stream of water Johnson had been playing on the worst of the fire seemed to have an effect, and with a malignant hiss the main part of the blaze subsided.

"We're all accounted for." Jess's gaze swung from Tye, now giving the mare a slap on the rump that headed her and her foal away from danger, to where Bradley was taking the hose from an exhausted-looking Paul Johnson. "Which means whoever's still in there must be the bastard who set this fire."

He shook his head. "If it were up to me I'd think twice before risking my life or the life of anyone else here to try to save the scumbag. But fifteen years ago my old buddy Tye never had to look behind him to know I was backing him up. I guess some things just don't change."

His shoulders lifted ruefully. The next second he was moving toward the barn, and, looking ahead of him, Susannah saw Tye doing the same.

Her chest constricted in fear, but even as she saw Jess draw alongside his companion both men halted. Horror filled her as she saw what had stopped them.

The fiery and barely recognizable shape of a man staggered from the barn, the screams that had been issuing from his throat rising in pitch as he ran. Tye and Jess started forward in unison, but as they reached for him he shrugged them off with the same frantic strength the maddened horses had exhibited earlier. Tye shouted something, and Susannah saw Kevin Bradley redirect the powerful jet of water coming from the hose in his hands toward the burning man.

The blast was enough to knock him off balance even as it extinguished the flames engulfing him. His last two stumbling steps brought him to within feet of her before he fell to the ground.

He wasn't going to live, she realized immediately. No one could, after suffering the burns he had. Her first recoiling reaction to the sight of him fled, and with it any thought of blame for the evil destruction he had wrought here tonight. Whoever he was, whatever he had done, he was minutes—possibly seconds—away from answering for his crimes to a higher power than any to be found in this world, and he had to know that.

Without thinking she fell to her knees beside him and started to put out a hand, intending to touch him on his arm, but then she realized that there was no way of telling where his charred clothing ended and his flesh began.

"'The Lord is my shepherd....'"

They were probably the most familiar of all the old familiar words, but to her that had never robbed them of their comfort. Instinctively she went on, her voice barely audible.

"'I shall not want. He maketh me to lie down in green pastures: He leadeth me beside the still—'"

"Dammit, that's Vince Rosario. He had a brother here." Bradley's tone was hard. Looking up in momentary distraction, Susannah saw him standing over her and the burned man. He thrust his face closer. "You used your little brother as a lookout on your second-storey jobs until he got caught and was sent to the Double B to be straightened out, right?"

"Please." She cast a beseeching glance at the hired hand. "This isn't the time."

"Rosario showed up once to spring his brother out early. Del told him if he did, Tommy would have to serve the rest of his sentence in juvenile detention," Johnson corroborated. He looked at Tye uncertainly. "Should I call an ambulance?"

"He's past that," Tye said quietly. Hunkering down beside Susannah, he nodded at her. "Go on if you want, but I doubt he can hear you."

She shook her head somberly. "That doesn't matter, Tye." She lowered her gaze to the man Bradley had identified as Rosario, intending to continue, but to her shock he opened his eyes.

"Sister?"

The one-word query was little more than a painful croak, but the desperate urgency in Rosario's tone was unmistakable. After only the slightest of hesitations she gave a tiny nod.

"'Beside the still waters,'" she said softly. "'He restoreth my soul.'"

"The valley of the shadow of death." A terrible rasping sound came from him, but whether it was a laugh or a sob it was impossible to tell. "I always said I wouldn't be afraid when my time came, but I was wrong. I'm afraid, Sister. I want to make confession."

"You—you need a priest for that," Susannah said helplessly.

He gave no sign of having heard her. "Tommy didn't want to have any part of me when he came back from here—said his time at the Double B had showed him he could do something worthwhile with his life. I blamed Hawkins for turning him against me and I swore I'd make him pay for what he'd done."

"You were the one who attacked Jimmy Smith?" Tye's expression darkened. "You caused the accident that injured the senator's nephew?"

Rosario's gaze lost focus and he drew in an effort-filled, rattling breath. "I made a deal with the devil, Sister," he gasped. "Is it too late for me? Can you still say a prayer for my soul?"

Susannah saw Tye frown, saw him open his mouth to question the man further. Swiftly she forestalled him. "Of course I'll pray for you," she promised, compassion flooding through her. "We'll pray together. You know the words, don't you?" She picked up where he'd left off. "'I will fear no evil, for Thou art with me. Thy rod and Thy staff, they—'"

"He's not finished, Sister. He won't stop until he's destroyed everything." To her dismay she saw he was trying to lift himself up on his elbows. "He wants the baby, too, and he's—"

He fell backward. "He's *back*," he whispered hoarsely. "Tell Hawkins the old people were right— Skinwalker's back. And he's stalking again."

For a second longer his gaze remained locked on hers, as if he was willing her to understand his cryptic message. Then she saw one final, shuddering spasm pass through him, saw the last pinpoint of light in his eyes flicker and extinguish.

"He's gone." Despite what he'd said earlier, Jess sounded shaken. "Hell of a way to die."

"Aren't you forgetting something?" Bradley asked sharply. "That son of a bitch just tried to burn the place down. I say he got what he deserved, dammit."

Ignoring them, Susannah scrambled to her feet. Running back across the yard to the SUV, she wrenched open the door of the vehicle, her heart pounding so hard she could barely draw in a breath. Danny looked up solemnly.

She swept him into a fierce embrace. Behind her she heard a footstep, and she whirled around to see Tye standing there. Before he could speak she attacked.

"What baby, Tye? What other baby is there at the Double B?" Her words shook with unconcealed fury. "There *isn't* one, is there? Danny's the only baby here!"

"Suze, calm down for a minute and listen to me." As he spoke he took a step toward her. Swiftly shifting her son to a one-handed hold on her hip, she put up a shaking hand to keep him away.

"Rosario said he wants the baby. That has to mean he wants Danny." With an effort she steadied her voice, but she did nothing to soften the implacable accusation in her tone.

"I need to know what's going on, Tye, and I need to know now. Who's the Skinwalker…and what does he want with my *son?*"

"SKINWALKER'S just a legend."

She didn't believe him, Tye thought in weary frustration—no more than she'd believed him the previous half-dozen times in the past three hours that he'd said the same thing. But why should she? This whole mess was no one's fault but his, and since Vincent Rosario's dying words had revealed to Susannah that the man she'd trusted hadn't been entirely honest with her, it seemed she'd decided she couldn't accept anything he said. He tried a new tack.

"You tell her, Jess. Remember the stories we used to scare ourselves spitless with around the campfire when Del had us out riding herd? Remember Old Man Morgan warning us about the walking stones and the canyon ghost? Hell, even when we were kids we didn't really buy into any of it."

"Gabe Riggs did," Jess said unhelpfully. Tye glared at him and the other man shrugged defensively as he poured himself another cup of coffee, rejoining a silent Susannah at the kitchen table. "Well, he did, no matter how he pretended to scoff at the old beliefs. One day he couldn't find that piece of turquoise he always carried, and he said if he didn't find it by nightfall Skinwalker would come looking for him. Maybe that's why he hasn't shown up here yet."

"He hasn't shown up because Del hasn't been able to locate him," Tye growled. "Apparently Riggs quit

Recoveries International and dropped off the face of the earth after that hostage-rescue fiasco last year. Virgil Connor hasn't been able to get away, either, but all that means is he can't just walk out in the middle of an official FBI investigation to help an old friend, no matter how much he'd like to. That's not the point."

He tried to meet Susannah's eyes but deliberately she looked away, and the gesture, small as it was, made him feel even more like a heel. When he continued his tone was rougher than he'd intended.

"Del put out the call to a few of us ex-Double B's, Suze. He said there'd been trouble and he was worried it might escalate to the point where he'd have to shut down the ranch, or at least send his current crop of boys home early. In the end that's exactly what he did," he sighed, raking a hand through his hair. "A young Navajo horsebreaker who worked for him was found unconscious and badly beaten on the west quarter of the property, and right after that there was an accident involving one of the teens. With only a week or two before the end of their time here, he felt he couldn't take the risk."

Immediately he realized how badly he'd put it. He knew what she was going to say before she spoke.

"Like you risked my baby, Tye?" Her refusal to meet his gaze had stung, but the cold glance those golden-brown eyes now flicked over him cut like a whiplash. "Sheriff Bannerman offered to arrange protection for me and Danny, and without even consulting me you turned him down. I'd like to think your past history with him didn't have anything to do with that, but whatever your reasons, they weren't good enough."

She took a breath. "You say this Skinwalker's a legend—a bogeyman only little ones would be frightened by. It appears to me Del Hawkins put some stock in the story, if he called on you, Jess, and this Gabe Riggs and Virgil Connor you're talking about." She frowned. "You were all sent to the ranch as teens?"

"Virgil was a street fighter. Gabe hot-wired cars. Tye was an all-round general hell-raiser." Jess grinned sheepishly. "Me, I was an angel by comparison. I just hacked into computer systems to see if I could."

"You hacked into your school's computer and changed all your friends' marks to passing grades— for a price," Tye corrected him. "Who knew then your criminal expertise with computers would eventually be put to good use? Crawford Solutions," he added in response to Susannah's blank expression. "Its software is in every computer in the country."

"A self-made millionaire," Jess agreed complacently. "Nerds rule." His grin disappeared as quickly as it had appeared. "But if it hadn't been for Del, things would have turned out a whole lot differently for all of us, Susannah—which is why Tye put his bodyguard business in California on hold when he heard the ranch was in trouble, and why I came as soon as I could. I'm only glad to have had some small part in putting a stop to the incidents."

"A stop?" Although it was Jess's last comment she was responding to, Tye saw the dark honey gaze turn his way again. "How do you figure the incidents have stopped, after what Vincent Rosario said? The man was dying. Lord forgive me, he thought I was the nearest thing to a priest he was going to get and he was making his final confession.''

"And he was out of his head not only with guilt, but with the pain," he reminded her, as gently as he could. "You're right, I should have told you how things were here and let you decide whether you wanted to take Bannerman up on his offer. But he's only got three deputies, and his two most experienced people had been assigned to gather evidence at Greta's, which would have left Billy Parker guarding you."

"Parker..." Jess's brow wrinkled. "Where do I know that name from?"

"Moose," Tye sighed. "Moose Parker. Remember that football game the Double B boys played against the locals the year we were here?"

Jess's frown was replaced by a disbelieving grin. "Hell, yeah. They figured all they had to do was point Moose in the right direction and he'd annihilate us, except somehow he got off course and ploughed into the goalpost in the first five minutes. He's a deputy now?" He shook his head. "No wonder Bannerman showed up alone to take down the particulars of the fire before the coroner removed Rosario's body."

"Tye filled you in on my situation, Jess, so you know I was married to a con man." Susannah's voice was soft, but Tye thought he detected an ominous undertone beneath the sweetness. "At least Frank Barrett didn't have a sidekick helping him out. The two of you are about as pretty a pair of snake-oil salesmen as I've seen, but I'm near running out of patience. I don't want to hear about the sheriff or someone called

Moose or a football game that happened fifteen years ago—I want to know why a man I watched die today used up his last breath in warning me against a legend. I want to know why a tough Vietnam vet like Del Hawkins took that legend seriously enough to mention it when he asked for your help.''

''Because Skinwalker's not just a legend to the people who lived in these parts long before I came along. I'd be a fool not to respect their culture.''

Tye jerked his attention to the doorway and the man standing there. Del, his ramrod-straight bearing more a clue to his military past than a hint of the disability that forced him to steady his weight on a cane, met his eyes before turning to Susannah.

An astonished Susannah, Tye noted with surprised curiosity. Her lips were parted and the gaze she directed at the lean man approaching her was wide—a far cry, he thought wryly, from the narrow look she'd been favoring him with only seconds ago. Seemingly his and Jess's stories about their former mentor had fired her imagination.

''I spoke with Sheriff Bannerman before I came here and he told me I had visitors. Brought me up to speed on the excitement I missed, too. We didn't have a chance to get introduced last night,'' Del said easily, extending his free hand toward her. ''I was away most of last week but before I left Tye told me he'd turned obstetrician on the highway, and that his bedside manner had been so bad his patient had taken off on him. Greta filled me in a little more this morning, until a martinet of a head nurse read her the riot act about getting some rest, so I feel I already know you. Susannah Bird, right? I'm Del—''

"You're Del Hawkins. I—I feel like I know you, too."

Susannah had pushed back her chair and was standing, her whole attention focused on the man in front of her. Tye frowned. After the fire she'd changed out of the dress she'd been wearing and into another before tending to a hungry Danny's needs, and now she was smoothing her palms on the well-worn cotton skirt as if she was nervous. The garment was shapeless—she'd seemed embarrassed when she'd explained earlier that she still couldn't get into the few pre-pregnancy clothes she had with her—but even under the excess fabric it was possible to see the tense set of her shoulders.

There's something going on here, he thought sharply. *Something about meeting Del has her on a knife edge, dammit. But why?*

He got his answer soon enough.

"You're the Lieutenant Hawkins who was part of Beta Beta Force in Vietnam," Susannah said unsteadily, "a four-man covert operations group. Up until nearly the end of that war the four of you were like brothers, and you each had a design of two bees fighting to the death tattooed on your left biceps. I suspect that's why you called the ranch the Double B."

Susannah's attitude had roused his interest, Tye admitted grimly, but the expression on Del's normally unreadable features riveted him. The older man's face seemed drained of all color, his gaze dark with some strong emotion. When he spoke his voice was rusty.

"I should have known. You've got his hair and his eyes, sweetheart. Your father—how is he? Does he know you're here?"

She shook her head, and Tye saw her lips tremble before she answered. "Daniel Bird's been dead and gone these fifteen years, Mr. Hawkins. My son bears his name now. But I'm sure he knows I went looking for you when trouble came on me."

She took a hesitant step forward. Before she could take another Del had wrapped her in a one-armed bearhug and was crushing her to him. Just as at that long-ago foaling, Tye was dimly aware that Jess was clearing his throat and averting his face, overcome by the same feeling he was experiencing—of having intruded on a private moment.

"My Granny Lacey said Daddy always told her and my mama that if they were ever in need of help and he wasn't there for them, they should look you up," Susannah whispered against Del's chest. "It's taken me a time to track you down...but here I am."

Chapter Six

"I usually take my after-supper coffee on the front part of the porch, but until we tear down what's left of the barn and raise a new one the view from here gets my vote."

Del settled back in one of the back verandah's rustic varnished-log chairs and exhaled. "I like to watch the sun setting over the desert, anyway. No matter how hectic the day's been, looking at all that space kind of puts everything back into perspective for a man."

Susannah, Danny snoozing in her arms, smiled. "That phone call to Greta helped, too, didn't it?" she said. "I know hearing her voice made me feel better. What time are you leaving in the morning to go visit her at the hospital?"

As she asked the question, from the front of the house came the sound of Jess's quick laugh and the diffident tone she already recognized as the one Tye used when he was wryly amused. She heard their footsteps mounting the porch steps and her heart skipped a beat or two in her chest.

Even when she'd taken him to task earlier today there'd been a part of her that had felt dangerously vulnerable, meltingly weak every time she'd met his eyes, she reluctantly admitted. She knew how foolish her reaction was. What she hadn't decided yet was if it was wrong.

The Reverend Peabody who preached at that church Granny Lacey and I attended in Ohio would have thought so, she thought, an unconscious frown creasing her brow. *He would have labeled what I'm feeling as simple carnal lust, and he'd probably say it was even worse because I'm a brand-new mama who shouldn't be thinking this way at all about a man.*

Tye came around the corner of the porch, his stride long-legged and easy, his gaze going immediately to her and Danny. He smiled, and all thoughts of the good reverend fled as heat filled her.

"Johnson and Bradley got the last of the horses rounded up and corralled. Paul said they seemed a little spooked, but none the worse for wear." Leaning back against the porch railing, Tye hooked his thumbs in his jeans pockets and crossed his booted feet at the ankles. "Any word from Bannerman yet?"

"He called just after you and Jess went over to the bunkhouse," Susannah said, wondering in embarrassed dismay whether the croak she'd heard in her voice had been audible to anyone else. "They've had no luck so far in identifying the shooter from Greta's garage, and the two who got away are still at large. He offered again to arrange some kind of protective custody for me and Danny if I wanted."

"And you said?" Tye's question was uninflected but his gaze sharpened on hers as he waited for her answer.

"I said if it was all the same to him, I'd be staying

here,'' she replied, her tone now firmly under control. ''After all, I was heading for the ranch last week when my car broke down and Danny decided to make an appearance a little earlier than expected. If Greta hadn't told me Del was out of town for a few days, I would have shown up at the Double B before now.''

''I don't normally escort the boys back to their homes, and leaving the ranch at this particular time wasn't something I was eager to do even with Tye here to keep an eye on things,'' Del said. ''But I owed the senator an explanation as to why I was returning his nephew in a walking cast. I contacted him again this morning and told him the man who'd been instigating the accidents had perished in a fire.''

Del shrugged. ''I told Alice Tahe that, too, when her granddaughter, Joanna, drove her over for a visit this afternoon.''

''Alice Tahe?'' Jess, his hair wetly slicked back, dropped into the chair next to Del with a grimace. ''God, I've had three showers today and I still smell of smoke. Is she the one we used to call Old Lady Tahe?''

''She's the one you boys called Mrs. Tahe, after I put a couple of you on latrine duty to teach you some respect,'' Del said dryly. ''She had her hundredth birthday this spring, although her granddaughter's sure Alice shaved a year or two off her age when she married her third husband. By the way, Susannah, Joanna's a registered nurse who runs a Navajo Nation new-mother's clinic. She said if you'd like to bring Danny in tomorrow, she could weigh him and give him his first checkup.''

''Her clinic's got a top-notch reputation. I'll drive

you and Danny there in the morning if you want," Tye said, before turning back to Del.

"What was Alice's reaction when you told her Vincent Rosario had been trying to get back at you for straightening his little brother out?" he asked idly. Extracting a small folding knife from his pocket, he snapped it open and squinted at something on his thumb. He saw Susannah watching him. "Splinter," he said briefly. "Stings like the devil, dammit."

His pose of unconcern was just that, she knew—a pose. Alice Tahe, Del had explained to her earlier, had been convinced from the first that the disturbing incidents at the ranch couldn't be attributed to any human agency. Steeped in the old ways as she was, she'd found it easier to accept a supernatural explanation.

"Every culture has its werewolves and its demons," Del had elaborated. "The Navajos have Skinwalker, an evil spirit who can take on any shape he wants. Some versions say he can bend others to his will—use them as his puppets, so to speak."

"Vincent Rosario said he'd made a deal with the devil," she'd said, still not reassured. "Legend or not, isn't it possible someone learned of his grudge against the Double B and helped him...someone with an agenda of his own?"

"Tye told me what Vincent said about Skinwalker wanting the baby, sweetheart." Del had taken her hands in his. "That's part of the myth—that he comes around at night and steals little children away. Rosario knew he was dying, and from what you say he was terrified his crimes would damn him. My guess is that in his guilt he seized on the local legend as a scapegoat, dredging up every detail he could remember about it to convince himself he wasn't as bad as he feared.''

His no-nonsense words had set her world to rights again and banished the last of her fears for Danny.

''Alice's reaction?'' Del's reply to Tye's query brought Susannah back to the present. ''She told me I was a fool. Then she demanded that her granddaughter take her home.''

''So she doesn't think it's over.'' There was frustration in Tye's declaration. ''That could lead to trouble down the road, Del. If the Skinwalker rumors persist they might be used as a smoke screen for anyone who wants to get back at you, just as Rosario used them. I know not everyone around here's happy with the Double B taking in hellions who're one step away from jail.''

''But that's the way it's been since Del first bought this place,'' Jess interjected. ''At least Rosario's out of the picture now, and we can concentrate on Susannah's problem. Have you told her what I proposed?''

Tye shook his head, his somber expression changing to a one-sided smile. ''I thought I'd let you run it by her. You're always complaining I never let you be the hero in front of the girls.''

''And I'm right, dammit. After delivering Danny by the side of the highway, already you've got me playing catch-up.''

Jess's easy grin belied his aggrieved tone. He leaned forward in his chair, his gaze suddenly serious.

''As I understand it, Susannah, these people who've been tracking you were responsible for the death of your husband. That's how this whole thing started, right?''

"With Frank's murder, yes," she agreed, unconsciously tightening her hold on Danny. "It's like I told you and Del today—until then I'd never come in contact with any kind of violence at all."

"Except for your grandmother's death a few weeks previous to your meeting Barrett," Tye pointed out. "But that was an accident, you said."

"A hit-and-run." She frowned at him. "For heaven's sakes, Tye, you're not saying my grandmother's the key to what's been happening. She was a law-abiding, church-going older lady who was never involved in anything shady in her whole life. How can you suggest even for a minute that somehow she got on the wrong side of a bunch of professional killers?"

She was more incredulous than angry, Susannah thought, meeting his gaze. In fact, if the underlying subject wasn't murder, his theory would be laughable.

He folded the small knife he'd been holding and slipped it back into his pocket. "You're right," he said smoothly. "I guess the fact that the police never found the driver responsible for the accident sticks in my craw, but a lot of hit-and-runs go unsolved. Go on, Jess—you were saying we're pretty sure the answer lies with Frank Barrett. The thing is, we don't know much about the man."

"Which is where I can help," Jess continued. He looked uncertainly at Susannah. "If you want me to, of course. It would mean digging into your husband's past and there's no telling what we might find."

"Wait a minute." Del was shaking his head. "The authorities would have done that already. If they didn't find a clue as to who killed Frank Barrett and why, what makes you think you can?"

"Because I've got resources that law enforcement agencies can only dream of," Jess said without arrogance. "Technology that hasn't been released yet, software that won't go on the market for another couple of years, cutting-edge equipment most police forces just can't afford. That's what Crawford Solutions is all about, Del. Give me a day or so and I'll be able to provide you with a complete bio on Frank Barrett, including anyone he might have associated with. Tye can take it from there."

"It'd give us something to go on, Susannah." Restlessly Tye pushed himself away from the porch railing. "We're working in the dark here. For some reason it wasn't enough just to kill Frank and leave it at that—you were targeted as well. But until we figure out why he was murdered we can't do much except sit back and wait for the next attack. That's not the way I operate."

"It's the way I've been operating for the past nine months," Susannah said slowly. "I've been running like a rabbit with a pack of redbone hounds on its tail, but sooner or later the hounds always catch up to the rabbit."

She looked down at her son, sleepily snuggled against her breast. "My boy's not going to grow up scared and on the run. If your investigation into his daddy's past brings to light something I'd rather Danny didn't ever know, I'll figure out how I'm going to deal with it when he's older. You go ahead and run a check on Frank, Jess."

"I was counting on you saying that." Jess's good-looking features broke into a swift smile. He glanced at his watch and stood, his posture resolute. "I've already packed my duffel bag and stashed it in the utility. It's a three-hour drive to my little spread, so if I make tracks now I'll be able to start working on this tonight.''

She opened her mouth to protest, but he held up a hand. "You're saving me from another day in the great outdoors. Del'll tell you, I never really cut the mustard as a cowboy, but give me a windowless room and a bank of computer monitors and I'm a happy camper. As soon as I learn something I'll be in touch.''

If Jess Crawford and Tyler Adams were representative of the kind of men the Double B molded, Susannah thought as Del and Tye left her briefly to see Jess off, she could understand why the Vietnam vet had resolved to do everything in his power to combat any threat to the ranch. From what Jess had told her, Del's request for help had been unprecedented, and that in itself had signaled his desperation when he'd finally contacted four of the Double B's graduates.

"He's a good man, Daddy,'' she said under her breath, laying her cheek on the top of Danny's head and breathing in the baby scent of him. "Granny Lacey said he saved your life more'n once over there in that ripped-apart country, and you saved his a couple of times in turn. I'm glad you sent me to him.''

"I'm glad, too, sweetheart.''

Opening her eyes, she saw Del had returned and was watching her. Greta had called him her tough old mustang, she recalled, and there *was* a rawhide strength and toughness to the man. Not only did it display itself in the way he'd overcome a physical disability, but it was demonstrated by his dogged determination to salvage young lives before they were forever ruined.

He's cut from the same cloth Daniel Bird was, she thought as Del lowered himself stiffly into the chair beside her. *And Tye's a lot like both of them.*

"I should have kept up the friendship, Susannah. It was my fault your father and I lost touch with each other."

His tone was low and he'd leaned back in his chair, his eyes reflectively closed as hers had been only moments ago. When he sighed, to her ears there seemed to be a world of regret in the sound. Danny stirred in her arms, but although she shifted her hold on him she remained silent, knowing instinctively that the man beside her had more to say.

"There were four of us, as you know. Myself, your father, John MacLeish and Zeke Harmon. Beta Beta Force. I didn't name the ranch after us, by the way." She saw a gleam of gray as one eye opened a slit and glanced her way. "It was already called the Double B. I bought the place partly because of the name, though at the time I couldn't admit that to myself."

Booted footsteps signalled Tye's approach. As if he sensed Del's mood he merely nodded as he joined them, again choosing to stand instead of taking a seat. Unexpectedly, the realization came to Susannah that if she were both deaf and blind she still would have been somehow aware that he was nearby, although this time her awareness of his presence wasn't as edgy and heated as it had been previously. This time the feeling filling her was one of completeness, as if part of her had been missing and was missing no longer.

Like an unbroken circle, she thought, disconcerted

by the notion. *Me and Danny and Tye…it seems right, as if that's the way it should have been all along, and as if that's the way it should be from now on.*

She realized Del was speaking again. Not exactly sure why she felt so unsettled, she focused her attention on what he was saying.

"We were a band of brothers, and the tattoos were a symbol of how we felt. I think it was Zeke who came up with the idea, John who sketched it out and me who requested a few days R and R for us in Saigon, where we all trooped into a tiny tattoo parlor and got them done. Two killer bees fighting to the death. You've seen it, Tye."

"Your left biceps. I've seen it." The corners of Tye's mouth lifted. "It impressed the hell out of me when I was a kid. I wanted one just like it, but even then I knew it was something more than just a design."

"A long time ago, maybe." Del's eyes were open now, and he looked down at the cane lying on the porch by his feet. "Now that's probably exactly what it is. I'm the only one left, and not all of me returned from that war."

He wasn't only talking about the disability that had robbed him of his legs, Susannah knew. The pain in his voice went too deep.

"Zeke died over there," Del said in an undertone. "A few days later I stepped onto what looked like a patch of bamboo shoots in a swamp and the world exploded around me. When I woke up in a stateside hospital weeks later they told me the war was over and a friend of mine was waiting to see me, but neither one of those two pieces of news meant anything to me.''

His grin was crooked. ''I sent him away, Susannah. Your father kept coming back. Finally I told him that seeing him made everything worse, and he stopped visiting me. It was years after that I came across his address written on the flyleaf of a book he'd given me, but I couldn't contact him. I was too ashamed of the way I'd treated him.''

''What happened to MacLeish?'' Tye's eyebrows drew together. ''Did he make it out?''

''Five years after hostilities officially ceased.'' Del's gaze darkened. ''You ever hear of MIA bracelets? Missing in action,'' he added in response to Susannah's look. ''Plain silver, with only a name, rank and date engraved on them, the date being when the MIA in question had last been seen. I saw one once with John's name on it. For five years he was kept in what they called a tiger cage, with the outside world not knowing if he was alive or dead. Finally he was released.''

''He's not the same MacLeish who went into politics, is he?'' Tye's query was sharp. ''Married a young Vietnamese woman, was rumored to be in the running as his party's candidate in the next senatorial race about ten years ago before he—'' Abruptly he stopped.

''Murder-suicide makes a pretty sensational news story, doesn't it?'' Del said heavily. ''I hear some tabloid television show had their pet psychiatrist come on to explain how those years as a prisoner must have snapped something in John's mind that eventually led him to kill his wife before drowning himself. I prefer to remember him as the patriot and comrade-in-arms he was when I knew him. I would have gone to his funeral if his body had ever been recovered.''

Abruptly he reached for his cane. ''Hell, we were four scared-spitless kids who'd been dropped into a country and a situation we weren't sure we could handle. I guess the tattoo was our way of whistling past the graveyard, except the graveyard got everyone but me in the end.'' He stood. ''You know, I hear they've got lasers nowadays that can remove tattoos.''

With a small start, Susannah realized that dusk had fallen while they'd been talking. Velvety shadows pooled in the far corners of the verandah, and Del's expression was obscured.

''Guess I'll check on the horses,'' he said, his tone a signal the conversation was at an end. ''I'd better make sure that foal's settled down from all the excitement.''

He was almost at the end of the porch before she called to him. Roused by the sound of her voice, Danny awoke and opened his mouth in an enormous yawn, staring in sudden fascination at Tye. Susannah's gaze rested lovingly on her son before she lifted her eyes to Del.

''It still stands for something, that tattoo the four of you got all those years ago.'' Her voice was firm and clear. ''It stands for a bond that never broke, Del. Maybe you lost touch with my father and John Mac-Leish, maybe you're the only one who survived, but what those fighting bees symbolize still holds true. It brought Daniel Bird's daughter and his grandson halfway across the country to your doorstep. You didn't even think of turning us away. I hope you don't get it removed.''

For a moment Hawkins didn't reply. Then his shoulders squared, and she saw the brief flash of his smile in the gathering dark. ''Maybe I won't, at that. After all, it seems this ranch produced the next generation of Double B men, doesn't it?''

He turned the corner of the porch and disappeared from view. A second later she heard the sound of his walking stick steadying him as he made his way down the steps to the yard, now illuminated with the lights he'd flicked on.

''I'd be willing to bet there's more to that story than we learned tonight,'' Tye said. He took a step toward her, his manner offhand. ''How about I hold him for a while, Suze?''

Surprised, she blinked at him. Then she recovered. ''He'd probably love it if you did. I don't think he's taken his eyes off you since he woke up.''

Carefully she handed Danny into his arms, and blinked again as he cradled the tiny body as deftly as if the action was second nature to him.

''He—he smells a little milky,'' she said, slightly embarrassed. ''To me that's just contented-baby smell, but—''

''It's contented-baby smell to me, too,'' Tye said, bending his head to Danny's clutching fingers. A tiny palm brushed against the stubble of his jaw. ''I like it. I can always tell when you've just fed him.''

''It's not exactly French perfume.'' He wasn't just talking about Danny, Susannah knew. She'd noticed that same milk-and-talcum-powder baby scent on herself more than once. He raised an eyebrow.

"No, it's not French perfume. And the Frenchman who discovers how to bottle anything that erotic is going to be a very rich man, honey," he said blandly. Before she could react he went on. "I've always suspected Del had his ghosts, but tonight they were stronger than ever. I'm glad you said what you did."

"I just told him the truth."

"*The next generation of Double B men...*" His tanned lips curved into a slow smile. "You know what the locals always said this place's initials stood for, Suze? Bad Boy Ranch. More appropriate, don't you think?"

"Maybe fifteen years ago, but not now," she protested. "For heaven's sakes, you dropped everything when you learned Del was in trouble and now you've taken on my problems, too. Jess barely knows me and yet he's using Crawford Solutions's resources to find out what he can about Frank."

He shrugged uncomfortably. "Hell, we're no heroes. Just working off some serious karma, honey—trying to make up for all those cars we hot-wired and those street rumbles we got into when we were wild and crazy and out of control. I think Dan the Man's about ready for some shut-eye. I'd better hand him over to his mama again."

For a moment as he gently transferred the small, warm body into her embrace, both of them were holding Danny. The feeling of completeness, of *rightness* again struck Susannah, as it had done earlier.

And this time she knew what it meant.

The Reverend Peabody would have been wrong, she thought shakily. What she felt for the big man with the baby in his arms wasn't mere lust and it wasn't just physical, although physical was part of it.

She was falling in love with Tyler Adams…and even an unsophisticated single mama from Fox Hollow had to know a relationship between her and a fast-living, sweet-talking, ex-bad boy would *never* work.

Chapter Seven

"Once in a while Frank would say he'd left his wallet in his other jacket and ask me if I could spot him for breakfast at the diner," Susannah said, staring at the rutted road ahead of them and barely noticing as the truck bounced jarringly in and out of a pothole. "Other times, it was all I could do to convince him it wasn't fitting for him to buy me an expensive watch or a pair of earrings. I don't know why I didn't figure out before now that only a gambler could practically throw money away one day and be flat broke the next."

Jess had phoned early this morning, just shortly after Del had left for the hospital and while she was getting Danny ready for his outing to Joanna Tahe's clinic. Tye had taken the call and it had been left to him to break the news to her—news that obviously hadn't been a surprise to him, however shocked she'd been by it.

"Atlantic City—" he'd shrugged "—and a grifter who liked fast money he didn't have to work for. It seemed likely he wasn't there for the salt air."

"How did Jess find out all this so fast?" she'd

asked. "He must have been on the computer all night, but still…"

"Despite the laid-back impression he likes to give, Jess can run rings around most of the high-paid geniuses he's got working for him," Tye had informed her. "He used some experimental software Crawford Solutions recently developed. After he downloaded one of Barrett's old mug shots the program compared it with newspaper photos, surveillance videos, pictures from the security cameras in automatic bank machines—you name it. In this day and age, everybody's on file somewhere. He got about a hundred hits, and at least half a dozen of them were from casino videos."

She'd frowned. "Most of this is beyond me, Tye, but I wouldn't have thought private surveillance pictures would be available to just anyone with a computer."

"Fifteen years ago our boy Jess was capable of hacking into school records," he'd said with brief humor. "Let's just say I figured it was best not to ask too many questions."

He'd gone on to tell her the rest of what his friend had learned—that not only had Frank been a gambler, and an unlucky one, but he'd been blacklisted from several of the more well-known casinos for not making good on his losses.

"After he was barred from the mainstream operations he went to the mob-run joints," Tye had said. "In particular, he shows up several times on the surveillance videos of Michael Saranno's club, and it's rumored that although Saranno poses as a legitimate businessman he has his own way of dealing with deadbeats and cheats. There's a real possibility Frank's death was a mob hit, Susannah.''

One day in the future Danny would want to know everything she could tell him about his father, Susannah thought now, glancing over her shoulder at her son in his infant seat as they jounced over another patch of bad road. She wouldn't lie to him, but she would make sure he knew there had been more to Frank Barrett than the unpalatable facts Jess had gleaned from his computers and software. She looked down at her hands, lacing her fingers together in her lap.

''I only saw him lose his temper once,'' she said. She felt rather than saw Tye take his attention from the road for a second and look at her, but she didn't meet his eyes.

''A waitress who worked with me broke up with an abusive boyfriend, and the boyfriend showed up at the diner. Frank had him out of the door so fast his feet barely touched the ground, and when he took a swing at him, Frank laid him out cold in the parking lot. That was one of the times he was flush. When he came back into the diner he gave Lydia all the money he had on him and said she should make a new start in another city. Whatever else a body might say about Frank, he couldn't abide seeing a woman being threatened like that. It would have torn him apart to think he'd been responsible for what's been happening to me and Danny.''

Now she did meet his gaze, her own clouded with worry. ''This Michael Saranno—how does Jess figure he's going to get in to see him?''

It had been the final unwelcome component of

Jess's theory that a reluctant Tye had relayed to her this morning. If the killers targeting Susannah were mob hit men who'd eliminated Frank Barrett as an object lesson to other gamblers, their pursuit of her could mean Saranno intended to drive his warning home with a vengeance: not only would prospective deadbeats be putting themselves in jeopardy, but their families would be punished, as well. Jess had felt their only hope of calling off Saranno's thugs would be for him to approach the mobster personally to plead Susannah's case. Minutes after his conversation with Tye he'd boarded his company jet with the intention of doing just that.

"Crawford Solutions does business with some of Saranno's legitimate enterprises." Tye winced as the washboard surface of the road gave way to unstable gravel. "And Jess isn't certain Saranno will agree to see him, he just thought it was worth a shot. So do I."

He flicked a glance into the rearview mirror at the baby in the back seat, the lines around his mouth relaxing slightly. "Joanna Tahe said the word had already spread around the reservation about me delivering a baby by the side of the road. The women at her clinic were joking that the Double B would make a good maternity hospital."

If he'd meant to divert Susannah with his change of topic he'd succeeded. She smiled swiftly. "From what you've told me about her I can almost imagine her talking Del into it, at that. It was good of her to offer to check me and Danny over, Tye."

"I know Doc Jennings in Last Chance isn't an option as long as we're trying to keep a low profile for you and Danny, but if you'd prefer I took you into Gallup to see a doctor—'' he began, but she didn't let him finish.

''You said Joanna spent ten years in Albuquerque as a maternity ward nurse before returning home here to open a new mothers' clinic. It sounds like Joanna is way more qualified than any wet-behind-the-ears young doctor I might get if I just showed up at a hospital with Danny in my arms, and besides, we agreed it's probably safer to stick as close to the ranch as possible until we hear from Jess.''

She looked at the passing landscape with interest. ''When do we cross over into the reservation?''

''We've been on Navajo Nation land since shortly after we passed the Double B's boundary. We're talking a fair chunk of real estate, Suze...bigger than West Virginia,'' he added with a teasing smile, gearing the truck down. ''This slice of northwest New Mexico is only a small section of it—the *Dinetah* crosses into parts of Arizona and Utah, too.''

He saw her puzzled look and elaborated. ''The Navajos' name for themselves is *Dineh*. It means the People, and *Dinetah* means Navajo country, or homeland. There's the clinic, just ahead.''

It was a squat white building, seemingly plunked down in the middle of nowhere. Three or four pickup trucks were parked nearby, one with a brindle-coated mongrel sitting in the driver's seat, waiting for its owner. As Tye swung in to park alongside the vehicle, a dark-haired man in his late twenties or early thirties appeared from around the back of the clinic. Seeing their approach, he halted, his expression closed but not unfriendly.

''Joanna's brother, Matthew,'' Tye informed her in an undertone. ''He'll give us a good reason for running into us here, but my guess is he planned it this way because he wanted to see you for himself. Matt's Tribal Police.'' He shot her a wry glance. ''Just the fact that the unknown *Belacana* woman everyone's talking about who gave birth at the side of the highway chose to bring her baby to his sister's clinic, rather than going to an anglo doctor, would have him interested.''

Belacana, Susannah surmised, had to mean non-*Dineh*. It was the second time he'd referred to the gossip surrounding Danny's unconventional birth, and she felt sudden alarm.

''This is what I was afraid of,'' she said tightly as the truck came to a stop and Tye switched off the motor. Out of the corner of her eye she saw Matt Tahe walking casually toward them. ''If anyone's asking around about me and Danny, it won't take long before they find out everything they need to know, including where we're staying. I know you said the Double B's secure, but Vincent Rosario got past Kevin Bradley two nights ago, Tye, and my best chance of keeping my little boy safe was making sure no one found us.''

''Rosario had to have gotten onto the property while Kevin was occupied with Jess,'' he said with a frown. He nodded at Matt, now only a few yards away from them. ''Even if your presence here is an open secret among the *Dineh* and the tribal authorities feel they should check you out, don't worry. A stranger asking questions won't get any answers from the People.''

"Tyler Adams. It's been a long time since you paid the Four Corners a visit."

Joanna Tahe's brother drew near as Tye alighted from the truck. He didn't offer his hand, Susannah noted as she opened her own door and flipped back the seat to unbuckle Danny, and she was glad Tye had explained earlier this morning to her that the omission was customary and not to be taken as an insult. But that was as far as her peace of mind went, she thought worriedly, scooping a wriggling Danny into her arms. How could she be sure Tahe wouldn't mention her presence over coffee in a café, or that one of the mothers at the clinic wouldn't inadvertently let something slip the next time she was in town buying formula?

"Too long." There was faint surprise in Tye's voice, as if he'd just realized his answer held more truth than he'd realized. He repeated himself, more slowly this time. "Too long. I'd almost forgotten what clean air smelled like."

"My second cousin works out in California," Matt said, nodding. "Stunt work for the movies. He says it's hard to keep to the Way when some days you can't even see the sky for the smog. But the money's good, Joseph tells me."

It wasn't quite a question. It wasn't just a comment, either, Susannah sensed.

"Your second cousin's right, the money's good if that's all a man's interested in. The people who hire my security firm to guard them certainly have all the toys and the possessions."

Tye seemed to have fallen into the same unhurried and thoughtful cadence as the black-haired man he was talking to. He looked away, narrowing his eyes at the horizon. Automatically following his gaze, Susannah saw that although the sky above them was cloudless and blue, the far-off ridge of mountains shimmered hazily.

''Thunderheads building up.'' Tahe's observation was directed at her, and for the first time he smiled. ''Sometimes tourists don't realize how fast the road can wash away in a flash flood. I'll have to keep my eyes peeled for strangers, I guess, warn them off for their own good.''

''I heard once of a pack of wild dogs getting swept away.'' Tye shrugged. ''Damnedest thing. But they'd been hanging around a herd of sheep trying to get at the lambs, so it was just as well. Saved the price of the bullets it would have taken to eradicate them.''

Susannah felt suddenly at home. The conversation, convoluted as it was, would have made perfect sense to Granny Lacey or to any other close-lipped Fox Hollower, she thought with an inward smile. Even the fact that Tye hadn't introduced her to Matt Tahe was significant—he'd wanted the lawman to realize he was aware Matt knew perfectly well who she was, and that their supposedly accidental meeting here was no accident.

Whatever doubts Tahe might have had about Tye and the woman he was protecting had been dealt with in the same roundabout fashion. Tye had made clear his respect for the Way Tahe had spoken of—the Navajo Way of moderation and balance she remembered Del mentioning during one of their conversations yesterday—and in return Tahe had pledged his cooperation in watching out for any suspicious strangers.

It's like the stories Granny told me, about the gov-

ernment men who used to come around looking for Jeb Wainwright's still during Prohibition, she thought, amused and reassured at the same time. *They never did find it. Even folks who didn't hold with bootlegging wouldn't have told on Jeb.*

"...on my way to his hogan to speak with him now. You're welcome to come if you want." Matt Tahe was speaking again, his manner diffident. "Of course, if Alfred Nez really does believe it was a witch he saw in the canyon two nights ago he'll be too afraid to say much of anything useful, but we might learn something from him."

"Your grandmother isn't too scared to let everyone know she thinks there's a Navajo witch on the loose," Tye said evenly. "She was at the Double B yesterday, warning Del that the Skinwalker was still stalking."

"My sister told me," Matt said, his expression darkening. "Grandmother also thinks that as long as she carries some pollen in a pouch she can keep Skinwalker away. She won't listen to me when I tell her that if she's wrong and it was an ordinary man who killed those horses we found last week and Billy Morgan's sheep the month before that, nothing in a medicine bag could protect her if he thinks she knows something and decides to silence her."

"I knew about the horses. I thought it was an isolated incident, maybe someone getting revenge on the owner for something they thought he did." Tye exhaled sharply. "I hadn't heard there'd been other incidents besides the ones at the Double B."

"Not related, I'm sure." Tahe shrugged. "When we catch whoever's responsible it'll probably be the same kind of scenario as what was going on at Del's

ranch with Vincent Rosario—someone with a griev-
ance, out to cause as much trouble as possible. Still,
until we catch him I'd feel better if Grandmother was
more careful. You want to come with me to see Alfred
Nez? We'll be back within the hour.''

''Go on, Tye,'' Susannah said, seeing his indeci-
sion. She nodded at the other pickups parked nearby.
''Seems as if there's other ladies ahead of me, so I'll
likely be here a spell. No point in you waiting in the
truck for me, and you might feel a little out of place
with the mamas and the babies inside.''

His slow grin told he'd been thinking the same
thing, but over her protests he insisted on escorting
her into the clinic before leaving with Matt, seemingly
unaware of the silent flutter of interest his brief appearance in the waiting room had caused.

Unaware, or so used to it he didn't notice anymore,
she mused half an hour later when the last mother and
child went into the examination room with an apolo-
getically smiling Joanna Tahe, leaving her alone for
the moment with her thoughts. From the joking comments Jess had made, even as a teen Tyler Adams had
been irresistible to the opposite sex, and the broad-
shouldered, good-looking man he'd become since
wouldn't ever have had any trouble attracting women.

But probably not all of them were fool enough to
fall in love with him, she thought heavily, rocking an
uncharacteristically fretting Danny in her arms. *And*
you haven't just fallen for him, have you? You actually
lay in bed last night wondering what it would be like
being married to the man, for heaven's sakes.

He'd kissed her—once. In her world that meant
something, but in the circles Tye moved in—in the

circles a lot of other people moved in, Susannah reminded herself—a kiss didn't have to mean anything. Even sleeping with someone didn't have to mean anything.

Except it does to me. She looked down at Danny. *Sleeping with someone has to mean you're willing to accept the possibility you might make a baby with them. That's a commitment, in my book.*

"A lifelong commitment, at that," she murmured to her son. "Which means marriage. I know a lot of folks don't think that way these days and I'm not saying anything against them, but I guess I was brought up kind of old-fashioned, little man. I'm not his type of woman at all, am I? I never could be, not in a million years."

And if she was, she suspected it wouldn't make a pinch of difference to Tye. *I don't believe in much of anything…* She'd seen beneath the hard surface of the words he'd spoken the other day, and guessed what he'd left unsaid: …*not even myself.*

He'd known instinctively how guilty she'd felt over not loving Frank—known and related to that guilt, because by his own admission he'd felt it, too.

He's never fallen in love, she thought suddenly. *He'd like to—maybe that's why he told me he'd wished he could change, become another kind of man. But he knows himself well enough to admit that he can't…and likely for the same reason I can't change who I am. I was raised by Granny Lacey to believe in marriage. Tye was raised by a man who saw it as a contract to be broken.*

"So this is the young man who decided to be born

in the back seat of a car. It doesn't appear as if it did
you any harm, but your mom looks a little peaky.''

At Joanna Tahe's gently teasing words, Susannah
hastily fixed a smile to her lips and received an answering smile from both Joanna and the woman heading out the door with the sturdy, black-haired baby in
her arms. The ex-maternity nurse exchanged goodbyes
with her patient before turning back to Susannah, her
glance keenly assessing.

"You're my last before lunch, so we won't have to
rush,'' she said, leading the way to the examination
room opening off from the small reception area. ''I
like to have mom and baby weighed first and then I'll
do physicals on the two of you, but I always think the
most important part of this primary exam is for you
to feel you can talk with me. About anything,'' she
added, handing Susannah a clean backless smock and
taking Danny from her. ''Fortunately, I've found that
walking around with your rump exposed to a total
stranger seems to break the ice pretty darn fast.''

This last was delivered with a wry grin, and the
slight awkwardness Susannah had been feeling evap-
orated. Twenty minutes later as she finished getting
dressed again, she found herself chatting with Joanna
Tahe as if they'd been friends forever.

"I was pretty sure he was doing just fine, but it's
good to hear it from a professional. His weight's
right?''

"His weight, his development, his everything.''
The other woman hesitated. ''And physically you've
got nothing to worry about, either, but I hear you've
been living with more than a little stress for longer
than you—''

Joanna broke off with a frown at the sound of the clinic's outer door being opened and closed. With a swift apology, she got to her feet and went out to the reception area, and a moment later Susannah heard her speaking rapidly and firmly in Navajo to her visitor, but whatever it was she said, it didn't have the desired effect.

"*Nali,* please. You can't go in there!"

The woman who appeared in the open doorway, followed almost immediately by Joanna Tahe, had to be Alice, her grandmother, Susannah guessed. Her face, as wrinkled as a walnut, was framed by hair that, despite her age, was still the color of a moonless night, pulled into a tight bun at the back of her head and bound by white yarn. Unlike the other *Dineh* Susannah had seen this morning, Alice wore some semblance of traditional Navajo garb, although, despite the late-May warmth, topping her many-tiered skirt and her silver-buttoned, velveteen blouse was an olive-drab safari-type jacket. Granny Lacey's incongruous note had been a pair of high-cut sneakers she'd taken to wearing with her support hose and her neatly ironed dresses, Susannah remembered with affectionate amusement. But as strong-minded as Lacey Bird could be at times, it seemed as if Alice Tahe had her beat hands-down in the stubborn department.

Her granddaughter shot Susannah a look of frustration before speaking firmly to the old woman. "*Nali,* this is a medical place and the examination room is private. I told you Matthew and I would come to your hogan for lunch today. We're having stew and fry bread, remember?"

In their nest of wrinkles, obsidian eyes snapped angrily and Alice Tahe shook off her granddaughter's restraining hand. "I remember. I cooked the mutton myself this morning."

She pointed at Susannah, the heavy turquoise bracelet she wore sliding up her fragile-looking wrist. "You're the one the Skinwalker wants, *Belacana*— you and your boy-child. What did you do to him, to make him hate you so?"

"*Nali,* that's enough!" There was a thread of anger in Joanna's voice, but beneath the anger Susannah was sure she heard fear. "Matthew has told you there is danger in speaking so publicly of these things, and I am telling you not to frighten my patients in such a manner. I have respect for the old ways, Grandmother, you know that. But you said it yourself—Susannah is not of the People and this can mean nothing to her. Now, please, you must go."

"I'm not *Dineh,* no." Holding Danny tightly to her, Susannah stepped in front of Joanna before she could take her grandmother by the arm again. "I'm from a place called Fox Hollow, Mrs. Tahe, but your granddaughter's wrong. This Skinwalker you're talking about—he's pure evil, isn't he? Whatever name a body calls him by, my own granny taught me to watch out for him when I was just a little girl."

Alice Tahe nodded, and her wrinkled lips stretched into a thin smile. "I know, *Belacana.* Your grandmother was in my dream last night. She told me to warn you."

"Granny Lacey?" Shaken, Susannah stared at the old woman. Then she shook her head, but before she could say anything Alice Tahe went on impatiently.

"She wears shoes like the ones the young boys

wear.'' She shrugged. ''But she came at the end of my dream. First I saw Skinwalker, hiding in the desert watching you and your newborn son.''

''I'm sorry, Susannah.'' Joanna's gaze was dark with concern. ''You don't need this on top of everything else you've gone through—''

''No. No, let her tell me the rest of her dream,'' Susannah said shakily. ''*Nali,* did Skinwalker say what he wanted with me and my child?'' Unconsciously she used the term of respectful affection Joanna had addressed her grandmother by, and the obsidian eyes watching her softened.

''He told me nothing. He didn't know I had entered his world until the smell of the woodsmoke on my clothes came to his nostrils, and then he was angry. He tried to turn on me, but I was protected.'' Alice Tahe's voice had been steady enough, but now it quavered. ''He said he had killed many men, and he had enjoyed killing them. He said you and the child are part of the debt his enemies—''

Her words broke off and her gaze widened fearfully. Her hand went immediately to a small leather pouch at her waist, and the next moment Susannah saw the thong it was attached to snap into two strands.

The open pouch fell to the floor, a drift of bright golden pollen spilling from it.

''*Nali!*'' Joanna Tahe rushed to her grandmother's side just as the old lady's legs gave way. ''*Nali,* you must lie down. Let me help—''

''Get away from me!'' Alice Tahe's words weren't directed at her granddaughter, Susannah realized, but at someone or something only she could see. Her breath was a labored gasp. "Get away from me, Skin—"

A terrible spasm of pain contorted her features. The hand that had been fumbling for the leather pouch flew to her chest before falling again to her side, her head slumping back bonelessly on her neck.

"Her heart." Joanna Tahe lowered the frail body to the floor, the worry in her voice mixed with professional decisiveness. "She's been having pains lately. I can start CPR but she needs to get to a hospital, except Matt gave me a lift to the clinic today and I don't have my truck here."

"Where's your telephone?" Swiftly laying Danny in his carry-cot, Susannah turned to the door leading to the reception area, but her companion stopped her.

"The phone's out today. Whenever there's a storm brewing we seem to lose service." Already she was unbuttoning the silver-coin buttons on the wine-colored velveteen blouse. She looked up worriedly. "We can't wait for my brother and Tye to return. Can you go for help, Susannah? Jimmy Rock's trailer's just down the road."

She only wished she could do more, Susannah thought as she hurried from the clinic a few minutes later. The attack Alice Tahe had suffered had been a direct result of her determination to warn the *Belacana* of danger, and her agitation had proved too much for her.

You shouldn't have encouraged her, she told herself guiltily. *Why did you?*

There was no easy answer to that question, she admitted. As she'd told the old lady, she knew full well that evil existed—the last nine months had proved that beyond a shadow of a doubt. But as Tye and Del had insisted, Skinwalker was just a legend. The threat that had followed her here was a human one and if Jess Crawford was right, that human threat was called Michael Saranno.

"I'll admit she has the gift," she gasped out loud to herself, rounding a bend in the road and seeing the trailer home Joanna had spoken of. "Plenty of folks have second sight, or just plain get feelings they can't explain away. Maybe she can even read a body's mind, even if she doesn't know she's doing it. I was thinking of Granny Lacey's high-tops right before she mentioned them."

Her foot slipped on a loose stone and a stabbing pain shot through her left ankle. At the same moment, the dark clouds that had been massing overhead gave an ominous rumble, and instantly the rain came pouring down.

It was like stepping into a waterfall, Susannah thought, blinking rapidly against the rain but then giving up and settling for peering through her half-closed lashes. Trying not to put too much weight on her left foot, she half stumbled, half ran toward Jimmy Rock's trailer. In her urgency she didn't see the pothole until she was upon it.

This time her misstep was disastrous. It also, she was to reflect thankfully hours later, probably saved her life.

Because, as she fell face forward into the craterlike depression, she felt a sharp tug, as if something had suddenly torn the sleeve of her dress, and heard the flat and deadly sound of the rifle that had just been fired in her direction.

Chapter Eight

They hadn't learned anything from Alfred Nez because Alfred Nez hadn't been at his hogan when they'd arrived, Tye thought in mild annoyance on the drive back to the clinic to pick up Susannah. Alfred Nez, they'd eventually discovered, had left early this morning on a spur-of-the-moment trip to visit his daughter in Window Rock. Unfortunately this information had only been gleaned after forty-five minutes of roundabout conversation with Nez's nearest neighbor, Charlie Smith, who, if he wasn't quite Alice Tahe's age, was pretty close to it, and like many elderly, lonely people was inclined to be garrulous when he had a captive audience.

Over glasses of some sickly-sweet lemon-lime soft drink Matt Tahe had patiently discussed with Nez's neighbor the pros and cons of using a medicinal dip against ear mites in Charlie's small flock of Churro sheep, the benefits, if any, of the Navajo Nation being granted statehood as some felt it should be, and Charlie's disgruntled opinion of the younger generation of the *Dineh*. Charlie's niece's son was a wild one, Tye had gathered from the old man's disgusted dismissal of the boy.

"He skips school and listens to crazy music," Smith had grunted, pouring another round of lemon-lime soda. "He acts like he has no relatives."

Among a people who held family connection to be all-important, Tye knew this phrase was used only to convey serious condemnation. But though his niece's son had apparently forgotten the old ways according to Charlie, it was obvious Matt Tahe's deferential manner had gradually won him over.

"Your sheep pen looks stout and secure," Matt had observed eventually, sipping his third soda with all evidence of appreciation. "But I saw a ewe full of milk with no lamb to feed. Was it too weak to survive?"

"It was carried off in the night." Charlie Smith's garrulousness abruptly dried up with Matt's question. "A coyote, perhaps."

"My grandfather, you know Alfred Nez has talked of seeing a Skinwalker in the shape of a wolf in the canyons not far from here. Now he has gone to visit his daughter in Window Rock, and I wonder if he left because he feared the witch had followed him here from the canyons. Was it a coyote that took your lamb from such a sturdy pen, my grandfather? Or was it a wolf—a wolf walking upright like a man?"

"I do not know, my grandson." Smith had addressed the younger man with the same respect that Tahe had shown him, but his gaze had slid away nervously. "I saw a shadow, nothing more. I had taken up my rifle when the sheep's screams woke me and I fired at the shadow, but although I was sure my aim had been good the shadow leapt away, taking the lamb with it.''

And that had been pretty much that, Tye thought now as Matt capably steered the pickup in a slalom course around the ruts and potholes on the road leading to the clinic. A man had thought he'd seen something in a canyon two nights ago. A lamb had been stolen. An old lady had seized upon a legend to make some sense of a few violent and frightening incidents.

And just before Greta Hassell had stopped her truck at the side of the highway last week, Susannah had felt the presence of evil threatening her and Danny.

That was more understandable than the rest. She and her son *were* threatened, and as Jess's digging had seemed to indicate, by a man evil enough to target an innocent woman because of a monetary loss.

Innocent. That was the word to describe Susannah Bird, all right. Sudden frustration washed through him and he exhaled more sharply than he'd intended.

She was innocent and she was good—good in the most basic meaning of the word, good to the very fiber of her being. She was uncomplicated, again in no sense of the word but the least elaborate one. She was unsophisticated, and if she had any of the pretty little tricks the women he knew used to pique a man's interest, she'd never taken advantage of them.

There was no damn reason why he shouldn't be able to look at her and feel nothing more than an altruistic and entirely laudatory desire to help her and her baby. But what he felt when he looked at Susannah Bird was about as far from altruistic as it was possible to get, and there wasn't anything laudatory about it at all.

He wanted to see that honey-brown hair spread out on a pillow—*his* pillow. He wanted her in his bed, he wanted to see those full, soft breasts that were always primly covered by those god-awful cotton dresses she wore, he wanted to hear that honeycomb voice of hers wrapping breathlessly around his name just before she lost all coherency, just before he lost his mind.

And he could bring her to that, Tye thought. Because the one word he wouldn't use to describe Susannah Bird was *straitlaced*.

She probably thought the Sunday-school exterior she projected was the real her. He knew women, and he knew better. Just below the surface there was a part of Susannah that was pure Saturday night, part of her that wanted him as much as he wanted her, part of her that could engage the devil in his own game and leave him begging for mercy.

She wasn't straitlaced. And if she didn't have any tricks, he knew them all, and had never seen any reason not to use them to get what he wanted. So having her in his bed didn't have to remain just a fantasy.

But a fantasy was all it would ever be.

Hell of a time to acquire a set of morals, Adams, he told himself disgustedly, *especially when you've gotten along fine without them up until now.*

He wasn't a player. More than a few of the relationships he'd been involved in had taken months to run their course, and one liaison had been almost as long-lived as some of the marriages his father had negotiated divorce settlements for. But forever wasn't in the cards—never had been, never would be. And despite the heat he knew was in her, Susannah would want not only passion from him but commitment.

"Hell, it would never last between us," he muttered under his breath. "If I've learned one thing from growing up with Marvin Adams, it's that. And when Danny starts thinking of some man as his father, the son of a bitch should be someone who's going to stick around."

"Damn straight," Matt agreed, shifting the truck into a lower gear. Tye looked sharply at him.

"Damn straight what?" he demanded edgily, pissed off with himself for speaking his thoughts aloud.

"Damn straight whatever it was you just said," Matt said mildly. "I didn't catch it all, but it sounded as if you were in no mood to have anyone arguing with you about it."

Tye glared at him suspiciously. A corner of Matt's mouth quirked up in a smile. Despite himself, Tye felt a rueful grin spread across his own face.

"Damn straight I'm in no mood," he answered. "Neither are you, right? You were hoping to learn something more concrete today, weren't you?"

"I wanted to learn enough to eliminate some far-fetched possibilities," Matt said slowly. "I didn't. I don't expect you to understand, Tyler."

"Good, because I don't." Tye raised his eyebrows incredulously. "You're not trying to tell me you seriously believe a man can turn into—"

He broke off abruptly as they rounded a last curve and the clinic came into view, blue-black thunderheads now making it seem as if the sky was closing in on the small building. But that wasn't the only difference from the scene he and Matt had left an hour ago. Now the parking lot was empty of trucks except for his and one other. Into the unfamiliar vehicle's covered back cargo bed two young men were carefully sliding what looked like a makeshift stretcher. The body on the stretcher wore a many-tiered skirt and, incongruously, a bush jacket.

"That's my grandmother!" Matt wrenched the steering wheel over and turned into the clinic lot even as the skies above them opened and the rain that had been threatening all morning came bucketing down. Bringing the vehicle to a skidding stop he jumped out, Tye close on his heels.

Alice Tahe—it was Alice Tahe, Tye saw as they reached the two young men and their burden—looked to be in a bad way, her skin ashen and her eyes closed. His first thought was that she'd suffered some sort of attack, and his off-the-cuff diagnosis was immediately confirmed by Joanna Tahe as she exited the clinic.

"Matthew!" She hastened through the pouring rain to her brother, her features carved in tense lines. "I think Grandmother's had a heart attack. I got her stabilized, but she needs a doctor." She inclined her head toward the two young men. "Tom Dove and his friend dropped by to tell me Tom's wife can't make her appointment this afternoon. Tom's driving me to the hospital with *Nali,* but I didn't know what I was going to do about Danny."

"What do you mean? Where's Susannah?" Too late Tye realized he'd barked the questions at the woman, but she seemed to understand his concern.

"Nothing's happened to her. She's gone up the road to get—"

The rest of her sentence was lost as the unmistakable sound of a rifleshot rang out, so loudly that it felt as if it was splitting the very air around them. Tye froze.

The next moment he was sprinting toward Matt's vehicle.

"Adams, wait! This is police business." Matt caught up with him as he swung himself into the driver's seat and turned the key in the ignition. The motor roared to life.

"I don't think so. Susannah's safety is my business," Tye said hoarsely. "Besides, there may be more than one shooter on the loose, and someone has to stay behind to guard Danny. Get out of my way, Matt, or I'll—"

"The shotgun's loaded. There's more ammo in the box under the seat."

Matt leapt from the truck's running board as Tye threw the vehicle into Reverse. Gravel flew up as he backed out of the parking lot and then shot forward, the engine racing as he sped down the road in the direction the shot had come from. One-handedly he unclipped the short-barreled shotgun from its cradle on the floor beside the seat.

He'd been so sure, so *criminally* sure nothing could harm her here, he berated himself, pushing the accelerator pedal to the floor and correcting the truck's progress as it started to slide into a skid. Strangers found it hard to pass unnoticed on the *Dinetah,* and he'd counted on that to discourage Susannah's pursuers from targeting her while she was with Joanna Tahe.

He was lying to himself, he thought coldly.

"That's not why you went off with Matt chasing ghosts and witches that didn't exist, Adams, and you know it," he said to himself between clenched teeth.

"Sure, you let your guard down because you were on the reservation but admit it—you were glad of the excuse to get away from her. Just being near her is driving you crazy…and you can't *stand* feeling that way, especially when you know there's nothing you can do about it."

A second shot rang out. Rounding a bend in the road, through the pelting rain he saw a splash of color against the gravel up ahead—a splash of blue and white, like the blue-and-white dress Susannah had been wearing when he'd left her at the clinic an hour ago.

Susannah was lying facedown on the road only yards away. Even now she could be dead.

The truck tires bit into the gravel and locked as he braked, but already he was out of the vehicle and running the last few feet to her. As he fell to his knees beside her she raised her head fearfully.

"Tye!" There was a nasty graze on her cheek and her face was smeared with mud, but all he could see was that golden-brown gaze, wide with apprehension. Relief flooded through him. "There's someone shooting at me, Tye. What are we going to do? I think he's somewhere in the trees behind that trailer, just waiting for us to make a move."

"Then his wait's over," Tye said harshly. "I have to get you out of here, honey, and the truck's our best bet. On the count of three, run. I'm going to be with you every step of the way, firing back at the bastard. One, two—"

"Tye, wait!" Her voice was thin. "If something happens to me—"

"I'm going to make damn sure nothing does happen to you—'' he began. She cut him off, her tone strained and urgent.

''If something happens to me I need to know Danny's going to be in good hands. Maybe this isn't formal or anything, but if you say you'll care for my boy that's enough for me. Will you, Tye? Will you look after Danny if…if his mama's not around for him?''

Her eyes, wide and pleading, met his. Something in him felt like it was cracking in two.

''You don't have to ask, Suze,'' he said huskily. ''But it's not going to come to that. Now, on my count run for the truck and don't look back no matter what. If I don't make it, head for the clinic and tell Matt what's happened.''

''Leave you behind? No, Tye, I couldn't—''

''*Three!*''

As he rasped out the command, he rose, jerking her up with him. Almost immediately he heard the flat whine of a shot, and, giving Susannah a push to propel her forward, he fired back in the general direction of the trees behind the trailer.

Out of the corner of his eye he saw her take a halting step. Her face went white with pain, and she came close to falling.

''My ankle,'' she gasped. ''I twisted it on my way here.''

''Hold on to me,'' he said swiftly, pulling her to him with his free hand and taking care to keep his own body between her and the hidden rifleman. ''Only a few more yards, Suze. Come on, you can make it.''

He didn't hear the shot that ploughed through his shoulder, and for an instant he didn't even feel it.

Then the pain bloomed, hot and wet and immediate. He ignored it. Forcing his arm up he pulled off another one-handed shot, all the while stumbling toward the truck with Susannah at his side. As they reached the vehicle's open door he boosted her up onto the seat.

"Scoot over, honey." He could barely recognize his own voice. "Take the shotgun and start firing out the window to keep him occupied."

She hesitated, and then grabbed the weapon from him, her expression set. He kept forgetting one simple fact, Tye thought disjointedly as he hauled himself behind the wheel and reached for the gearshift, glad it was his left arm and not his right that was useless. This woman had survived a deadly hunt that had stretched over eight states. Despite her gentle exterior, Susannah Bird had a core of forged steel.

"You're hurt!" Appalled dismay shadowed her eyes as she glimpsed the blood now soaking the left sleeve of his shirt. Her lips firmed to an angry line. "Keep him occupied? If he steps out from cover just once, I believe I'll do a little better'n that, Tye."

They were a regular Bonnie and Clyde, he thought lightheadedly as the truck slewed backward through the pouring rain at top speed, Susannah firing steadily. Her maneuver had the desired effect of allowing them to reach the curve in the road without further incident. Gunning the motor, he let the back end of the vehicle swing around in an unstable arc before taking the truck out of reverse and heading for the clinic.

As they neared the building he saw Matt Tahe about to get into the truck he and Susannah had arrived in, but as the Navajo lawman saw them he strode toward them, his relief at their return evident on his rain-wet features.

"The shooter was firing from somewhere near the house-trailer down the road. I took one of his bullets but I don't think any of mine hit him," Tye said without preamble as Tahe reached the truck. "He had damn good cover, so you're going to need me with you when you go in after him. If we can find something to strap up my arm I should be able to hold a shotgun."

He wasn't sure if that was true. His shoulder felt as if it was attached to his body with a rusty steel spike, and even the slightest movement seemed to drive the spike farther in.

"Jimmy Rock's place?" Matt looked grim. "There's a couple of accessible trails leading from his property. His son has a backhoe and Jimmy got him to carve out some extra roads, which isn't going to make my job any easier."

He glanced over his shoulder and Tye saw a Tribal Police vehicle barreling into the parking lot, a young policeman at the wheel. "And thanks for the offer, Adams, but judging from the look of that shoulder I'd say you're on the disabled list for the time being. Besides, I think the best thing you can do right now is to get Susannah and that little guy of hers back to the Double B. Your son's fine," he added to her. "A friend of Joanna's came by just after you left, and I put her on baby-sitting detail."

Tahe was a highly capable law officer, Tye thought as the Tribal Police vehicle pulled out of the parking lot at top speed. But he'd been right in his assessment of the situation—it wasn't going to be easy finding the shooter. As worrying as that was though, what concerned Tye even more was that the shooter had found *them*.

Encountering an unprotected Susannah by Rock's trailer had to have been nothing more a lucky break on the part of her assailant, but the fact remained that her would-be killer had obviously followed them onto Navajo land in readiness for just such a break. Up until now he'd been assuming the men who'd been hunting her since Frank Barrett's murder in New Jersey were hired enforcers; good at what they did, certainly, but readily identifiable as what they were. He'd based that assumption on the man he'd taken out in Greta's garage, Tye acknowledged. Today had proven that assumption dangerously wrong.

One of the three who'd pursued Susannah to New Mexico had the ability to blend in with the local populace, at least to the extent that his presence here on the *Dinetah* had roused no instant suspicion. That was bad news, he thought grimly. In fact, the only bright spot in this whole disastrous day was that the lone gunman by Jimmy Rock's trailer had been just that— alone.

Which means the bullet you fired into his buddy the other night either put him out of the running for good or at least eliminated him as a threat for the time being, he told himself. *I wouldn't count on it being the former, Adams, given your dismal track record on this case so far.*

Greta's surgeon had said that she had to have had a guardian angel. That same angel must have put in some overtime today watching over Susannah, he thought bitterly, because her so-called bodyguard couldn't take any credit for her survival.

His hand on the door, he turned to her. "Matt's right, Suze, the Double B's the best place for you and Danny. One of Del's men can stand guard at the house itself while the other's stationed at the gate leading onto the property, and Del should be back from the hospital later this afternoon. With three able-bodied men on alert you'll be safe."

Cautiously he moved his arm, and bright pain stabbed through him. He ignored it and went on, seeing no reason to modulate the self-condemnation in his tone. "But it's up to you. I wouldn't blame you if you decided not to accept my assessment of the situation and tell Bannerman you've reconsidered his offer of protective custody. What nearly happened to you today was my fault, and I know it."

Susannah frowned. "What in the world are you talking about? That bullet you took was meant for me, Tye. You've saved my life twice now—maybe three times, because I don't know what I'd have done if you hadn't come by when I was giving birth to Danny."

Her face was mud-streaked and her hair was plastered wetly to her skull. Her dress was ruined. He kept seeing her at her worst, Tye thought. At her worst she still had every other woman beat hands down. At her worst she still had the power to make his heart turn over.

Gratitude was the last thing he wanted from her.

"I didn't save your life, I put it in jeopardy," he said harshly. "If that shooter today had taken me down it wouldn't have been any more than I deserved, honey.''

"Tyler Adams, you hush your mouth!'' Her eyes blazed with sudden fury. "For some reason being a hero doesn't sit well with you. That's just too bad, because from where I'm standing that's *exactly* what you are, so for heaven's sake get used to it!''

He stared at her, too taken aback to attempt a reply. She stared angrily back at him, her attitude so tensely electric it seemed as though the lightning outside had charged the air between them.

He always swore later that she cracked first. She always insisted he hadn't been able to hold back the grin that had broken her composure. However it happened, one moment the two of them were glaring at each other and the next thing Tye knew they were both laughing, Susannah so hard the tears came to her eyes.

And then the tears took over.

"Suze, honey, don't cry.''

He'd dated one or two actresses in his time, he recalled distractedly. Crying had been something they'd been able to do at will, and they'd looked heartbreakingly gorgeous while the tears had slowly slid down their faces. The same with the models he'd known— like liquid crystal, shimmering drops had trembled on their lower lashes, sometimes even splashing to their chiseled cheekbones. He'd always caved at the sight of female tears.

But he'd never felt like this—as though he would gladly tear out his heart and give it to her if by doing so he could take all her unhappiness, all her sorrow, away.

She didn't cry like a model, or like an actress. She cried like a woman.

"You could have been killed, Tye." She rubbed the heels of her hands across her cheeks, smearing the dirt into a paste. She shook her head, and fixed him with a red-rimmed gaze. "That's all I could think of while we were driving back here just now—you could have been killed, and I never would have gotten the chance to…the chance to…"

Her eyes squeezed shut and she pressed her lips together, as if to keep whatever it was she'd been about to say locked up behind them. Helplessly he touched her hair.

"I wasn't killed, Suze. But I died a thousand deaths when I thought something had happened to you." Desperately he searched for something that would take away the anguish in her voice. "Looks like we both got second chances at making sure whenever our time really does come we'll have done everything we wanted to in this life."

It had been the first thing he'd been able to think of, but it seemed he'd struck a chord with her. She opened her eyes.

"You mean without having to regret the things we didn't do," she said slowly, not phrasing it as a question. She looked at him, and beneath the mud on her cheeks he saw a faint touch of pink.

"I saw a greeting card once, Tye. It said, 'Life's a party. Eat cake.' Granny Lacey said it was foolish, but I…" She swallowed visibly. "I wondered if maybe eating cake wasn't sometimes just as important as everything else. Perhaps even more important, once in a while."

She'd grown up moving from town to town with a woman who, however much she'd loved her, couldn't have completely filled the place of the parents a five-year-old Susannah had lost so tragically, Tye thought slowly. And Lacey Bird's first priority would always have been to make sure she kept her dutiful grand-daughter's feet on the straight and narrow path, rather than unnecessarily smoothing that path for her. From what Susannah had said, they'd never had much money. From what she'd left unsaid, it was a good guess that any extra hadn't been spent on what Granny Lacey would undoubtedly call fripperies, but put in the collection plate or given to charity.

He'd never seen Susannah in anything but the cheapest of cotton dresses. The tiny collection of toiletries she'd lined up on the bathroom shelf at Del's were utilitarian bargain brands.

He didn't know what it was she'd been about to say a moment ago, but it wasn't hard to guess. If her life had been cut short today there was a world of things she wouldn't ever have experienced. He intended to set that right, starting now.

"Eat cake," he said quietly, looking at her and seeing the fugitive wistfulness behind that steady gaze.

There was a good possibility he wasn't the man for her. He knew that, although just acknowledging it came close to tearing him in two. She deserved someone better than Frank Barrett, someone better than Tyler Adams. She deserved a man who could believe in dreams and make them come true for her, and he wasn't sure he was that man. But whether he was or not, he was going to make everything up to her.

"Eat cake?" he repeated. He shook his head solemnly, his gaze holding hers. "That doesn't sound foolish to me, honey. That doesn't sound foolish at all."

Chapter Nine

"Miz Barrett, it's been too long since I had chicken-fried steak like that." Paul Johnson leaned back in his chair and patted his lean stomach. "And those mashed potatoes weren't anything like what we usually chow down on here. Del's pretty good at whipping the youngsters who come to the Double B into shape, but his potatoes usually end up a tad lumpy. He'll be sorry he missed this."

He gave a thoughtful shake of his head. "Or maybe not. As good a cook as you are, I guess his ladyfriend comes first with him. Can't blame the man for wanting to stay overnight in Gallup just to be on hand if she needs him."

"Great meal, Suze."

Tye was wearing faded jeans and a sweatshirt with the arms cut off, the better to accommodate his bandaged shoulder. Susannah knew the quick heat she felt touching her cheeks as she acknowledged his compliment wasn't solely due to pleasure that he'd enjoyed the food she'd cooked, and it didn't have anything at all to do with the fact she'd been standing over a stove. He raised his coffee cup to his lips, and the biceps she'd been staring at shifted slightly beneath the tan of his skin.

She snatched her gaze away. To her relief Paul Johnson spoke again, his tone more somber this time.

"The rez police didn't come up with any leads on the shooter? Seems to me like someone must have seen something."

"Tahe says not," Tye answered, frowning. "If these guys are mob hit men like Jess thinks, they should be sticking out like sore thumbs, but the shooter got on and presumably off Navajo land without raising an eyebrow."

"Matt's grandmother's going to be all right, at least," Susannah said. "When Joanna phoned she told me it hadn't been a full-blown attack, but more of a warning signal to the old lady. Not that Alice Tahe is taking any heed of the warning," she sighed. "Apparently she's more convinced than ever there's a ghost or a spirit behind all this."

"I'll keep my eyes peeled for a haunt, then," Johnson said, the almost unnoticeable crease in his cheek the only indication that his sunbaked features had briefly moved in a smile. He stood, and picked up a battered cowboy hat. "I'd better be getting along to my post. Miz Barrett, thanks again for the meal."

He was halfway to the door leading out to the porch before he turned back with a grimace. "Nearly forgot this." From the counter he scooped up a walkie-talkie and clipped it onto his belt. "I just hope Bradley's figured out the send-and-receive feature by now." He winked solemnly at Susannah, touched the brim of his hat in a sketchy salute to Tye and left.

"I hope he's figured it out, too," Tye said dryly.

He drained his coffee and set his cup down, one corner of his mouth quirking upward. "I get the feeling he's not happy about being pressed into service as security—he said something about signing on as a ranch hand, not a rent-a-cop when he took this job last month."

"Why exactly were *you* sent here, Tye? I know you said you landed in trouble with the law, but what did you do that was so bad your daddy washed his hands of you and packed you off to the Double B?"

Susannah saw the momentary tightness that passed over his face at her impulsive questions, and hastily she got to her feet. "Heavens, you must think I'm as nosy as an old spinster lady gossiping at the back fence. I'll just take care of these and then I should look in on Danny." She began to gather up the dishes, clattering them more than necessary to cover her embarrassment. "I'm sorry, Tye. I had no right to pry like that."

"Put the damn dishes down, Suze," he said mildly. When she didn't immediately comply, with his uninjured arm he reached over and lightly circled her wrist with his fingers. "I'll stack those in the dishwasher later. You weren't prying and I wasn't offended. I was just trying to think of a way to tell the story so I wouldn't come off looking like too much of a spoiled brat." He gave a one-shouldered shrug. "Except I couldn't."

Slowly she sat, her gaze uncertain. "A spoiled brat? I can't believe you were ever that awful, Tye."

"Believe it, honey." His grin might have passed for rueful if not for the swiftness with which it disappeared. "I grew up with a bigger allowance than a lot of people make putting in forty hours a week and overtime on a factory floor, and that wasn't counting the credit-card bills I racked up, no questions asked. I liked motorcycles. I liked driving them fast and driving them recklessly. God knows why I always walked away from the wreckage without a scratch, but I did. At one point even my father thought I needed to be taught money didn't grow on trees, and he cut me off without a penny.''

"What about your mama, Tye? You never mention her," she ventured cautiously.

"That would be because I never knew her. From the photos I've seen, she was quite a looker, which is probably why Marvin Adams ignored his own advice when he married her and skipped the prenup.'' His laugh was humorless. "Taught him a lesson he never forgot. All the rest of them had to sign on the dotted line before they walked down the aisle with him.''

"Oh.''

She wasn't going to ask him how many times his father had remarried, Susannah decided. Despite his offhand manner, it was obvious the subject was a painful one and she could understand why. Having two, or for all she knew, maybe three women succeeding his own mother—although even for California that number seemed to her unlikely—

"I can read you like a book, Suze.'' This time his smile, although slight, was genuine. "There were five after the first Mrs. Marvin Adams. Hell, no, I forgot Cheri. She only lasted seven months, but that was long enough for her to redecorate the Malibu house. Six.''

"Your daddy got hitched seven times?'' Her mouth

was open in an *O,* she realized. She voiced the query that was uppermost in her mind. "In a church?"

He looked surprised. "If they wanted a church wedding, sure. The way Marvin would have seen it, if it wasn't going to complicate the divorce later on, why not?"

"But—" She fell abruptly silent. *But what about the vows he would have taken?* she'd been about to say. *When he was standing in front of the altar, who did he think he was making those promises to?*

It wasn't fair to ask Tye to explain his father's actions, especially when it was clear there was a long-standing rift between them.

"You said you never knew your mama. She must have died not long after she and your daddy split up." Tentatively she laid her hand over his. "I'll bet she would have been proud of the man you grew into, Tye."

He turned his hand so it was palm up, and closed his fingers over hers. "Honey, you don't get it. This isn't a tragedy we're talking about here, it's a bedroom farce. Wendy Adams, née Halberstam, didn't die. As far as I know, she's still alive and collecting husbands—somewhere in Europe now, I seem to recall my father mentioning once. She wasn't the motherly type, so she didn't fight Marvin on custody. Hell, she didn't even press for access."

His tone was unconcerned. He gave her hand a quick squeeze and released it. "So anyway, there I was, sixteen years old and pissed off at the old man for shutting off the money tap. It didn't occur to me to get a part-time job. It occurred to me to steal the bikes I wanted to ride."

What would his reaction be if she interrupted him right now and told him how she felt about him? Susannah wondered, watching the blue of his eyes darken to indigo as he spoke, watching the way his expression changed when he spoke of his father. If she told him she'd fallen in love with him—not with the fallen angel she'd so fancifully imagined him to be when he'd first appeared to her, not with the devil she'd feared when she'd been overwhelmed by her own response to him, but with the man she now knew he was?

That man has his flaws, she told him silently. *You wouldn't be flesh and blood if you didn't, Tye. You're a hero, and a more decent man than you think, but you're awful good at lying to yourself. And because I'm in love with you I can see you're doing it now.*

He hadn't stolen motorcycles because he wanted the thrill of riding them. The rebellious teen he'd been all those years ago had broken the law in a futile attempt to gain the attention of a father who'd thought that throwing money at his son was an acceptable substitute for giving him his time and affection.

But the man in front of her obviously preferred his version, she thought. He'd sealed off that long-ago pain by denying it had ever existed, and maybe for him that had been the best way to deal with it.

The only trouble was, denying his past meant he'd never learn anything from it. One of these days, Marvin Adams's son would find that out for himself. For no reason at all, a tiny shiver of unnamed apprehension passed through her and from out of nowhere came a worried thought. *I only hope you do before it's too late, Tye…too late for both of us.*

She blinked, and focused her gaze on him as he went on.

"The first and second times I got caught my father paid to have the charges go away. The third time even his money wasn't enough to keep a lid on things, and I found myself in front of a judge being given a choice between cleaning up my act at a boot camp for teens called the Double B, or doing juvenile time. I figured the Double B sounded like the cushier gig. Del set me straight on that the day I arrived."

His grin was reminiscent. "Man, I hated him. We all did for the first few months—Connor, Jess, Gabe and me. But by the time our year was up and we had to leave the ranch, there wasn't a one of us who didn't know Hawkins had given us back our lives."

"So when he called asking for your help, you came," she said softly.

"When he asked for my help I came," he agreed. "So did Jess, and even though Rosario's no longer a threat I know Connor intends to pay Del a visit after he wraps up the FBI investigation he's on now." He raised a thoughtful eyebrow. "I said we all knew Del had given us back our lives, but now that I think of it, I'm not sure Gabe saw it that way. Even if Del's message had reached him I don't know whether he'd have shown up."

He fell silent for a second. Then he roused himself. "A bunch of tearaways. Who knew three of the four of us would end up in some variation of law enforcement? There's word Connor might make Area Director one of these days, for God's sake. I wish you'd reconsider what I suggested about bringing in the Bureau on this, Suze."

She shook her head decisively. "It would be like every other time I've gone to the authorities. You and Jess have done more to get to the bottom of this than the police ever have." She tried to keep her voice steady, but failed. "Oh, Tye, do you think anything will come of Jess's meeting with Michael Saranno tomorrow morning?"

Jess's phone call to them this afternoon had been brief, but cautious elation had colored his tone as he'd relayed the news that a face-to-face meeting had been arranged with the mobster.

"Just the fact that he's getting in to see the man is more than I'd dared to count on," Tye answered. "I'd like to tell you your troubles are over, Suze, but I won't lie to you. Saranno didn't get where he is in the mob by backing off just because someone asked him to. What I'm hoping is that Jess can make him see his reputation as a legitimate businessman will be ruined if it ever gets out he targeted a young mother with a baby."

"And until then, no leaving the ranch."

"Until then, no leaving the ranch." Tye shot her a quizzical look. "Why, was there someplace in particular you wanted to go?"

She sighed, and silently shelved a little dream that in her heart she'd known wouldn't really come true. "Danny's going to need more diapers in the next day or so," she fudged. "Maybe I can ask Del to pick some up on his way back tomorrow."

"Honey, do I smell a whiff of brimstone?" As she rose for the second time to clear the plates he again caught her hand, tugging her close enough to him so that she had no option but to meet his gaze. "Would that be a certain Mr. Scratch getting hold of your tongue? You didn't want to go into town just to buy diapers, did you?''

There was a glint of humor in his eyes. She looked away and down at her wrists, now both held by those strong hands.

''I knew I never should have told you about him. You're going to get after me worse'n Granny Lacey from now on, aren't you?''

She smiled in resignation. ''I took a notion it might be nice to buy a new dress, that's all. But my last waitressing job was in Texas almost a month ago, and I don't have much left of what I saved from my pay and tips. I'll probably just take in a couple of my maternity outfits—not that they'll need that much altering,'' she added in the spirit of unvarnished honesty. ''It'll take me a while to get back to anywhere near the size I wore before I got pregnant, and I never looked like those girls in the fashion advertisements in the first place.''

''Would you want to?''

His question didn't sound entirely casual, and suddenly her senses stirred into awareness. He was still clasping her hands in his—enclosing them, really, she thought faintly, since his grasp was so much larger. She could feel a slight line of callousing along the top of each of his palms, and she recalled him telling her that during the past week he'd been riding the Double B's fence line and helping Del with whatever needed doing around the ranch.

All it would take was a light tug from those hands, and she would tumble into his lap. She looked at him and belatedly realized she hadn't answered his question.

"Look like those girls?" With an effort she kept her eyes on his. "Have hair that gleams like silk, perfect pink nails, beautiful clothes?"

She attempted a little laugh that didn't get past her suddenly tight throat. "Have the kind of looks that would make a man fall in love with me at first sight?" she asked softly. "Just once I'd like to know what it felt like, Tye. Being one of those women, I mean."

"Would that be eating cake, Suze?" His voice was as husky as hers had been. A corner of his mouth lifted, but his smile didn't match the seriousness of his gaze. "You said earlier that if anything had happened to you today, you'd regret the things you hadn't let yourself do. That's what you meant, isn't it?"

How could she tell him? How could she tell him that he was partly right, and at the same time completely wrong? Something ballooned inside her chest until it was as if there wasn't room for anything else, not even the air that didn't seem to be reaching her lungs.

She was a plain-spoken woman, Susannah thought unhappily. She came from a long line of women who'd learned to face life and life's hard truths head-on. She didn't know how to make it sound fancy or pretty or sexy.

So she just said it plain.

"Eating cake would be letting myself go to your bed, Tye," she said, raising her chin and forcing herself to meet that heaven-blue gaze. "If I'd gone to meet my Maker today, I believe that would have been the one thing I'd have regretted never doing."

Chapter Ten

"I'm a new mama, of course." Pulling her hands from his grasp, she took a step backward and self-consciously smoothed down the full skirt of her dress with her palms. "Lovemaking's not something I'm going to be doing for a few weeks. But I wanted you to know how I felt."

She looked away. "The pretty clothes, the way those models in the magazines look? I guess I'd like to know how it feels to be the kind of woman who lives in your world, Tye...even if it was just for one night."

"But my world was empty."

She'd already begun to turn away when he spoke. She swung her gaze back to him, and was shaken to see the sudden bleakness etched on his features.

"I—I don't understand." She drew her eyebrows together in a puzzled frown. "You've made a success of your life, and on your own terms. How can you say your world is empty?"

"*Was* empty," he corrected her. "And I might have found some success, but I'm not so sure it was on my terms. If Del hadn't asked for my help, I would have come back to the Double B anyway, to see if I could figure out just how things ended up the way they did. I'd become my father, Suze. I'd lost touch with everything basic, everything real in life.''

He exhaled and raked a strong hand through the dark gold of his hair. ''Then I met you,'' he said simply. A smile ghosted across his features. ''A few minutes later, I met Daniel. And it was like I'd suddenly found my way out of a fog and into a clear blue day.'' He shook his head. ''Those size fours in the magazines? You're ten times more beautiful than they are. A hundred times more beautiful.''

''Oh, *no,* Tye.'' Her denial was immediate and aghast. ''That's crazy talk and you know it! I'm a mother and a working woman and I'm not ashamed of that, but I'm not blind. I cut my own hair. I keep my nails short because I can't be worryin' about them all the time. I don't believe I've ever felt silk against my skin, and—and—''

Wildly she cast around in her mind for something to end the discussion. ''For heaven's sake, Tye, I've never had one of those fancy perfumed bubble baths in my *life*. It's like trying to compare a Persian cat sitting on a cushion with a house tabby catching mice in the woodshed.''

Her clinching argument didn't appear to have clinched anything. His grin was swift, but even after it was replaced by a thoughtful frown she could still see the humor lurking at the back of his eyes. He got to his feet abruptly, as if he'd come to a decision.

''I want you in my bed, too,'' he said steadily. ''I can wait. No one knows better than I that you're a new mom, Suze, since I was there for the event.'' He reached out and pushed back a strand of her hair with a light finger. "But just because you gave birth a week and a half ago doesn't mean we can't make love, honey, because as far as I'm concerned the actual physical act's only one way of going about it. You know that shipment of supplies that got delivered today?"

Susannah nodded, and even that small movement seemed to require immense effort. She had no idea what he was talking about, she thought dazedly. She didn't care. She could stand here all night and just let that purr of his voice wash over her, feel the touch of his hand in her hair.

He wanted her. She didn't know why, but he wanted her. And even that revelation hadn't stolen her breath away, hadn't made her knees feel as if they barely could support her. He'd said he could wait…which meant that when he thought of the two of them together, he was thinking of a future.

"I lied." His words broke into her thoughts, but the momentary fear they aroused was instantly put to rest by his unrepentant smile. "They weren't ranch supplies at all, Suze. What that van brought from Last Chance today was a whole delivery of cake."

"Of cake?" He looked so pleased with himself a bubble of laughter rose up in her. "Now, Tye, even an unsophisticated Fox Hollow girl like me isn't gullible enough to believe that. You're teasing me."

"I'll prove it to you." Once again his hand wrapped around hers, and once again she felt as if whatever he wanted from her she wouldn't be able to deny him. "It's in my bedroom, honey."

Even as he took a first step toward the hall he stopped, the glance he gave her oddly uncertain.

"I know you weren't brought up to visit a man's bedroom with him, Susannah. Is this going to make you uncomfortable?"

They had a future, she thought. If they had a future then tonight, whatever it held, was the start of it and she wanted to start it right. She'd told him how she felt about him, but he didn't seem to understand how deep and how strong her feelings ran.

And he didn't seem to understand that although she'd been raised by Lacey Bird, she was her own woman.

"I'm not real experienced, Tye," she said, looking him straight in the eyes. "But I'm not a schoolgirl who doesn't know what it's all about between a man and a woman. I was married—maybe only for one night, and maybe to a man I found I didn't love, but I bore a son from that marriage. Today when I realized I could have lost you I did some hard thinking, and if I came to the wrong conclusion I guess the good Lord will let me know somehow."

She brought her free hand up, and softly touched his mouth. "I want to give myself to you. I don't see how any part of that could be wrong, as long as it's based on something true."

"It's true for me, Susannah." Somehow the fact that he used her full name made it sound like a pledge. "I did some hard thinking, too. I realized I wanted to give you everything I knew you'd never had."

They'd resumed walking, and as they passed the open door of her room Susannah glanced automatically in. Joanna Tahe had offered her the loan of a proper crib today during her visit to the clinic, and now it sat in the middle of the room, only steps from her own bed. In the pinpoint glow of a night-light she could see Danny sleeping peacefully.

Tye had been there at his birth. Tye had saved her and her son from the cold-eyed killer who'd been about to dispatch them both in Greta's garage. Today he'd laid his life on the line, not only for her, but for the baby he said had made all that was chaotic in his world fall perfectly into place.

He wanted to give her everything she didn't have, but what he didn't realize was that he already had, she thought tremulously.

He opened the door to his bedroom. Gently he propelled her forward with a hand on the small of her back.

"Just a minute." The room was in darkness and he reached for the light switch on the wall, but before he flicked it on he stopped. "Nah," he drawled. "Let's pull out all the stops, honey. Close your eyes."

Promptly, she did as he said, the lightheartedness that had risen in her before again bubbling up. If she'd been asked, she thought, she wouldn't have thought Tyler Adams could be playful. She'd seen the grimness in him and she'd seen the loyalty he felt for his friends. She'd known he could be an implacable opponent to those he went up against.

But right now she was seeing another side of him. It was the side that would be up before his children on Christmas morning, anticipating their delight and not wanting to miss a moment of it. It was the side that would place a squirming puppy in a son's arms and tell him it was his. It was the side that would stay up all night putting together a dollhouse for a daughter's birthday the next day.

"Okay, I guess you can look."

His tone was wryly amused, as if he knew he was indulging in foolishness and wasn't worried about it. She opened her eyes, and for a moment she didn't know what she was looking at.

He'd lit the oil lamp on the mantel over the fireplace. There was a smaller lamp glowing on a bedside table, and a third on the dresser, its soft yellow light reflected in the mirror behind it. Like the other bedrooms she'd glimpsed in the main house—Del had informed her that his yearly crop of teens bunked down like old-time cowboys in a separate building— Tye's room had a relaxed and masculine feel, with an obvious southwestern influence showing in the fabrics and furnishings.

But there was nothing masculine in the jumble of prettily wrapped and beribboned boxes spilling across the boldly patterned woven cover on the weathered log-pole bed. Hesitantly she drew closer. They ranged from tiny to a flat dress-box-sized one in violet-strewn paper. She turned an inquiring look on him as she picked up one of the smaller boxes.

"Who are these for?" Even as the question left her lips the answer came to her. "They're for Greta, aren't they? Oh, Tye, she'll love opening—"

"That's what I told the woman who owns Last Chance's one and only gift store when I phoned her this afternoon," he interrupted laconically. "Like everyone else in town, all she knew was that Greta had been injured during an attempted break-in at her home. I guess Bannerman isn't floating his drug-feud theory publicly yet, which might mean he's had second thoughts about it.'' He shrugged. ''Anyway, I told Lorraine they were get-well gifts from Del, and asked her if she'd have them wrapped and delivered here. They're for you, Suze. Start opening them.''

''They're for—'' As if it had suddenly become burningly hot in her hand, she dropped the box she was holding on to the bed. She sat down on the edge of the woven cover, her knees feeling as if they were about to give way. She found her voice again.

''I can't accept these from you, Tye. It—it wouldn't be right.''

She knew her objection sounded illogical. She'd told the man only minutes ago that she wanted to sleep with him, Susannah thought, and now she was refusing to accept his presents. *But it is different,* she told herself stubbornly. *I don't know why, but it is.*

''You know, I was pretty sure you'd say that.'' He jammed his hands in the front pockets of his jeans, and rocked slightly back on his heels. ''I hoped you wouldn't, but I figured you might. What if I told you they were your birthday presents, honey? Would that make it okay?''

''But it's not my birthday, Tye. My birthday's in March.''

''Better late than never, right?'' His grin flashed out, but he seemed to be waiting for her reaction.

Suddenly she knew how important this was to him. It was there in his eyes, it was in the studiedly unconcerned manner he was affecting, it was in the way he had sprung this on her, as if he'd hoped to melt her inhibitions with the element of surprise.

I want to give you everything you've never had.

There'd been a tenderness in his voice when he'd told her that. She picked up a squat, heavy box and pulled at the end of a curled ribbon.

"Life's a party, Tye?" She looked up at him, and saw the shadow behind his gaze disappear.

"Eat cake," he agreed softly. "Yeah, that's a good one to start with, Suze. Leave the biggest box for last, okay?"

It *did* feel like a party, she thought, carefully unwrapping the gift and feeling, in spite of herself, a building excitement as the paper fell away. Granny Lacey had always remembered her birthdays and Christmases with something she'd made herself, and every knitted scarf, every embroidered dresser runner, had been all the more valuable to Susannah because it had been created with love.

But there was something glamorous about getting a store-bought present, she admitted weakly. She pulled aside the final layer of paper and gasped.

"It's French," she said stupidly. She frowned up at him as if she expected him to deny it. "Tye, it's French, isn't it? French perfume?"

"As French as the Eiffel Tower," he said with a small smile. "But it's not just perfume. It's what Lorraine called a gift collection." He saw the sharp glance she gave him and his eyes widened in exaggerated innocence. "I was on the phone with her for half an hour, honey. We were bound to get onto a first-name basis at some point."

"It took popping out a baby in front of you for me to reach that same point," she said with mock tartness as she lifted the lid of the box. Even as she heard him laugh, she caught her breath again.

"After-bath veil? Foaming bath?"

"For that bubble bath you say you've never had."
He crossed his arms. "Plus a whole lot more stuff,
according to Lorraine. I don't know, maybe she got
carried away. Maybe you won't even like the scent.
She told me it was one of the lighter ones, and I
thought that would suit you."

Gingerly she uncapped a vial. Tipping it onto her
index finger, she dabbed quickly at the base of her
throat, behind her ears, on her wrists. She inhaled
deeply, her eyes closed in concentration.

"Oh, Tye, it's Fox Hollow." The unplanned words
came from her in a rush. "You—you gave me Fox
Hollow."

Her throat closed and she felt the tingle of tears
behind her eyelids. She opened them and looked at
him, blinking rapidly. "My mama had a clump of lil-
ies of the valley in her garden, and I remember her
putting a bunch in a water glass on my bedside table
once. She said they'd give me pretty dreams all night.
I'd forgotten that until now. This smells just like my
mama's flowers."

"You'd like to move back there, wouldn't you?"
he asked gently. "Do you still think of it as home?"

Carefully she put the bottle back in its allotted
place. She frowned, and slowly shook her head. "I'd
like to go back for a visit, and I think I still have kin
there. But you know, Tye, when I crossed over into
New Mexico I felt this was a place I could put down
new roots."

She put the box aside and picked up another one,
her gaze thoughtful. "I can't explain it. Maybe it's
because the sky seems so big here, or because there's

so much space. It's got everything—mountains and desert and grazing land and rivers. I believe I could live here.''

It was true, she thought in faint surprise. She hadn't put it into words before, but it was true.

''Could you live in California?''

His question was unexpected. Flustered, she pulled at the ribbon on the box in her lap. ''I—I've never thought about it,'' she said inadequately. She glanced at him through her eyelashes and saw he was watching her, his features unreadable.

''Then think about it, Suze,'' he said quietly. His expression lightened. ''But not right now. Right now I want to see you ripping open paper, lady.''

Her laugh was unsteady, and although she began opening the second present her thoughts were chaotic. It hadn't been a proposal, she told herself emphatically. She couldn't allow herself to think of it as a proposal. But if it hadn't been, what had he meant by telling her to consider it?

Her fingers were shaking, Susannah noticed.

''I went about that all wrong.'' His tone was edged. ''I told myself I wouldn't say anything to you until this whole business with Saranno was over and your life was back to normal. I'm asking you to take a lot on faith.''

''Like what?'' Her hands stilled.

''Like is there too much of Marvin Adams in me? Like would I end up being another Frank Barrett, someone you couldn't rely on in the long run?''

''You're taking a lot on faith, too.'' Slowly she set aside the box she was holding. Drawing a shallow breath, she stood, and took an unsteady step toward him. "Tye, what if I'm no good in the ways a woman wants to be with her man? On my wedding night, I didn't feel anything like I always thought you were supposed to. The earth didn't move. I just lay there, wishing it would be over soon."

She bit her lip uncertainly. "You—you said there were more ways of making love than just the basic act. I want to try some of those ways with you. I want to know that ten years from now, twenty years from now, you'll still find yourself in the middle of your day thinking about what we did the night before."

A few minutes ago he'd caught her off guard, Susannah thought. Now it was obvious she'd done the same to him. Under dark lashes, she saw his gaze widen briefly, and the blue of his eyes took on a deeper hue.

"You sure that's why you want to put me through my paces tonight, Suze?" he asked huskily. "It should be the other way around—you wanting to know if twenty years from now you're going to go weak in the knees thinking about how I was the night before."

Her mouth flew open. "No, Tye, that's not—"

"And I don't blame you one bit."

Easily he overrode her protest, and just as easily he bridged the slight distance between them. His right hand went around the back of her neck, sliding under the weight of her hair, and gently he pulled her to him.

"What if it's all just talk on my part, honey?" he murmured. "What if it never occurred to me to give you that bubble bath myself, to soap every satiny inch of you until you felt like you were on fire, and then to wrap you in the biggest towel I could find and carry you to the bed? What if I didn't even think of untying the silk robe you're going to take out of that big box over there, and stroking that perfumed lotion all over you? I could fumble the ball at any time, Suze. I think we'd better see just how well I can follow through on all this talk.''

Slowly—very slowly—he brought his mouth down. She felt his lips barely brush hers, but instead of taking the kiss deeper he let his tongue trail along the outline of her mouth. Somewhere inside her she felt a melting warmth begin to spread.

''When I first saw you I thought your hair looked like dark honey.'' His eyes were closed. He murmured the words against her lips. ''I wanted to feel it pouring through my hands and dripping onto my chest. I wanted to see it wet.''

''Already you're fumbling the ball, Tyler Adams.'' She let her own lashes drift closed, and the swirl of sensations inside her intensified. With an effort she continued. ''I think I saw shampoo in that fancy collection. Doesn't that give you any ideas?''

''I'm way ahead of you, sweetheart. You know, I'm glad that when Del renovated this place he added bathrooms for every bedroom.'' Against her lips she felt him smile. ''Next time I'll sweep you off your feet and carry you in, I promise. But with this bandaged shoulder I'm sporting today, I get the opportunity to watch that sweet butt of yours walking ahead of me, honey.''

Her eyes flew open as he made his point by giving her a light swat on her behind. He didn't immediately take his hand away, but let it linger on the curve of her derriere.

"You ever even think of going on a diet and losing this, and I'll never forgive you," he said huskily. "God, Susannah—don't you get it? I like it that you look like a real woman. This—" against her rump she felt his hands spread wide "—this drives me crazy. The way your hips flare out from your waist drives me crazy. I'd like to see you in something that clings to every rounded, sexy part of you."

She'd told him she wasn't experienced, Susannah thought, and that was true. But it didn't take a whole lot of sophistication to know what was happening to the man when just by holding her to him he was providing her with overwhelming evidence of his arousal. She felt as if her face was suffused with color. No, she corrected herself dizzily, she felt as if her whole *body* was blushing.

He took a step backward, exhaling raggedly. "Tell you what, Suze. I'll go run that bath for you. You put on that robe for me."

He didn't trust himself, she thought wonderingly as he left the room. Tyler Adams saw Susannah Bird as so desirable that he'd had to take a time-out, or risk losing that cool-edged, blond composure of his. She looked down at herself. He thought her curves were sexy. He wanted to let his gaze linger on them, let his hands cup them, see them without anything as inconvenient as clothing getting in his way.

She felt a sudden thrill of assuredness. She needed it when she unwrapped the largest box and shook out the gossamer folds of silk it contained. The accompanying tag slipped into the enfolding tissue paper described the material as sandwashed silk. In the room's soft lamplight, the garment's richly glowing tones of dark gold and old rose reminded her of a desert nightfall.

She felt wantonly exposed in it. True, it fell concealingly to her ankles, she told herself worriedly, and the deeply cuffed sleeves were roomy enough that she could slip her hands together in them like a muff. And there was nothing skimpy about the cut of the robe itself—it wrapped silkily around her with room to spare.

But the tie belt was of the same luxurious material. And silk against silk, she discovered as she cinched the belt around her waist for the third time, slid sexily apart almost as soon as she secured it.

Her courage faltered. She heard the bathwater in the adjoining room stop running, saw the half-open door swing back. Tye's eyes met her suddenly uncertain ones, and then his gaze took in all of her.

Hard color ran under his cheekbones. He didn't speak, but just stood there, as if he were drinking in the sight of her.

And just like that, all her doubts and worries faded to nothingness. She'd told herself from the start that they came from two different worlds, Susannah thought serenely. But that wasn't true anymore. She and Tye had created a world of their own.

Slowly she walked toward him, feeling silk against her thighs, silk brushing against her derriere. She knew without looking down that again the tie around her waist had loosened just enough to provide him with a tantalizing flash of creamy skin in the subdued glow from the dresser's oil lamp. As she reached him he moved aside to let her enter the bathroom, still without saying a word and still without taking his eyes from her. He'd opted for the same old-fashioned illumination in the spacious bathroom, she saw. On a small shelf over the sink was another glass lamp, its light warmly golden.

"You're beautiful." The words came out so hoarsely they were close to a whisper. He placed his hands on her shoulders and turned her to face him fully. "May I, Suze?"

The flickering light threw shadows against the hard planes of his features and emphasized the faint sandpaper texture stubbling his jawline. The muscles of his arms tensed, and without waiting for her reply he let his palms slide slowly down the silk sleeves of the robe to the tie around her waist. Hooking one finger into the looped bow, he released it completely.

The two edges of the robe slid open. Susannah felt the same scent-laden steam that was fogging the mirror instantly caress her.

If she'd considered it beforehand, she told herself, she would have thought she would feel shy. She was standing in front of him with nothing hiding her, nothing concealing her. She didn't feel shy at all, and only when Tye ran a light finger down the curve of a swollen breast did a slight self-consciousness assail her.

"They're the breasts of a nursing mom, Tye," she said softly. "Up until ten days ago this belly had a baby safe inside it."

He let his hand slide farther down, and when it got past her rib cage he spread his fingers. "I was just thinking the same thing," he said huskily. "I wish I'd been around then. I would have liked to have felt him growing in you.''

He raised his head. His gaze was so dark it might have been part of the midnight sky.

''I'd love to give you another baby, Susannah. When the time's right, I'd like to make a little brother or sister for Danny Tye.''

Chapter Eleven

"You know, Susannah, the Last Chance Café's been up for sale for a few months now. Anyone who can make meat loaf like this should seriously think of opening a place of her own."

At Del's words of praise, beside him Tye gave her a slow wink, unseen by the other occupant at the dinner table, Kevin Bradley. Susannah looked quickly down at her plate, pure happiness rushing through her.

She'd awakened in his arms this morning—in her bedroom, not his. He'd understood when she'd told him she couldn't fall asleep with a wall between her and Danny, even though with both bedroom doors open it had been possible to hear her son's slightest movement. At some time during the hours they'd been together Tye had stripped off his sweatshirt and jeans, and he'd put them back on with a wry grin.

"I'd feel better being able to watch over him, too, honey. I'll join you in a few minutes, but first I'm going to check in with Paul and Kevin and make sure everything's been quiet on the home front."

He'd pulled her to him and given her a quick, hard kiss before he'd left. He'd given her another when he'd returned and had slipped under the covers of her bed, snugging her tightly to his length. She'd drowsily opened her eyes to his good-morning kiss just after dawn, when he'd reluctantly left her to return to his own room.

Once during the night she'd come instantly awake, a moment later realizing that her motherly instinct had picked up on the quietly aggrieved hiccuping coming from the direction of Danny's crib. Before she'd been able to push back the covers and go to him, Tye had touched her shoulder.

"Let me, Suze. Poor guy, he sounds like he chugged back a couple of beers instead of milk at his last feeding."

Even as she'd stifled a giggle, he'd risen from the bed, pulled on his jeans for the second time that night and lifted Danny into his arms. As she'd drifted in and out of sleep for the next little while, every time she lifted her lashes the sight she saw had filled her with a kind of peaceful awe: a big man quietly pacing the floor, murmuring words she couldn't quite catch to the baby in his arms staring so solemnly up at him.

That was one side of Tyler Adams. Earlier he'd shown her another, and although that side had been equally tender, equally protective, he'd held back nothing of the heat and desire he felt for her. Heavens, who would have guessed a bath could be so erotic? Susannah wondered, feeling her breath catch as she relived every intoxicating moment. He'd lowered himself into the water behind her, a leanly muscled leg on either side of her thighs. Holding her close, he'd slipped lower in the tub, until her breasts had been two pink-tipped islands almost entirely covered with foam.

Her wedding night with Frank had been a hasty, fumbled affair. In contrast, Tye had brought a lazy, languid intimacy to everything he'd done with her—extravagantly soaping her breasts, slowly kissing the side of her neck, gently pulling her to him and whispering in her ear as she felt his hardness pressing against her.

He'd used the shower attachment to sluice clear water over her hair, and as the warm, needle-like spray had soaked through to her scalp she'd heard a purring sound of pure pleasure coming from somewhere deep in her own throat. Tye had heard it, too, and she'd known from his sudden tenseness that this evidence of her arousal had brought him dangerously near the edge.

Technically they hadn't made love, she thought now, smiling a secret smile to herself. But in the future they were destined to share, whenever she looked back on those hours they'd spent together she would count it as the night she and Tye had become lovers.

"Thanks for the grub."

As Kevin Bradley's curtly spoken words broke into her thoughts, Susannah saw he had risen from the table. She mustered some sort of reply, but before she'd finished speaking he'd already turned to Del.

"Mister Hawkins, I've been wondering if you could take a look at that gelding of mine I keep in the corral by the bunkhouse. For the past week or so I figure he's been favoring his left hind leg, but the damn thing won't let me get close enough to check it over."

"The past week?" Del frowned sharply. "Sure, I'll

take a look, see what's the matter with him. Why didn't you ask me sooner, for God's sake?''

Bradley shrugged carelessly. ''That horse never was worth half what I paid for him. I guess I was hoping whatever it was would clear up by itself, and save me the price of a vet bill. But it seems to be getting worse, so it looks like I'm either going to have to throw good money after bad or shoot him.''

''And that's not going to happen as long as the animal's on my property,'' Del said smoothly, but with an iron edge to his voice. ''Give me half an hour or so, Bradley. I'll bring hobbles and a twitch to keep him under control.''

''Could be a wire cut gone septic,'' Tye commented after the sound of Bradley's boots clattering down the porch steps had faded. ''Gotta tell you, Del, that guy just rubs me the wrong way.''

''You and me both,'' Hawkins grunted. ''I hired him and Johnson at the same time and I've never had to tell Paul anything twice, but with Kevin it's been one problem after another. He's not cowboy material, in my book. If I find he's let an animal suffer just because he didn't want to pay for its care, I'll be giving him his walking papers on the spot.''

''Does that mean you're going to rope me in to ride range? Dammit, Del, you know I've always said if the good Lord wanted us to sit on horses, then why would He have invented ergonomic chairs with adjustable backs?''

With a grin, Jess pushed open the screen door and halted at the threshold of the kitchen. ''I've spent all day catching connecting flights and I'm starving,'' he announced plaintively. ''Feed me.''

Already Susannah was heading toward the stove. "You poor man," she commiserated, her feigned tartness a cover for the butterflies that were suddenly filling her stomach. "I know what they serve at those fancy casinos—jumbo shrimp cocktails and filet mignon. How *did* you survive?"

"Hey—the lady got sassy while I was away." Jess pulled out a chair and plopped down in it. "Okay, here's the scoop, folks. Michael Saranno swears Barrett's murder wasn't his doing. I think he was telling me the truth."

He dropped his bombshell in the same light tone as his earlier banter, but as Susannah shot a startled glance in his direction she saw his expression held no humor. He grimaced, spreading his hands in a helpless gesture. "I don't know where that leaves us, but I get the feeling it's a place where a paddle might come in real handy. Saranno handed me one, but I'm not sure how reliable it is."

"How about we take it from the top again?" Tye said shortly. "This time slow down for the details, Jess. Michael Saranno swore to you Frank's death and the attempts on Susannah's life were nothing to do with him?"

"That's what he said. Thanks, Susannah, this looks great." As she set a plate of meat loaf and scalloped potatoes in front of him, Jess gave her a swift smile that held none of his usual jocularity. "I know this wasn't what you wanted to hear," he said gruffly. "I'm sorry I couldn't bring you more encouraging news."

"He's a mobster. Why should we trust him?" Tye's tone was disgusted.

"Because if he could have fessed up, he would have," Jess replied sharply. "He *wanted* to be able to give me what I was asking for—which was that he call off his goon squad and leave Susannah in peace. I was making him an offer he couldn't refuse, except he couldn't pony up the ante to accept my deal."

"What was your offer?" Up until now Del had been silent. Now his laconic question seemed to pull Jess up short.

"That I would shut down his casino operation." Suddenly the food on his plate seemed to require all his attention. He didn't meet Del's eyes. "And that before I did, I'd make sure the house had a run of luck so bad every player walked out a millionaire," he ended weakly.

"You what?" Tye stared at his friend. Then he gave a short laugh. "You son of a gun—there's a built-in glitch in the software you supplied him with, isn't there? Crawford, yours have gotta be made of brass, for crying out loud."

"You wouldn't believe how uncomfortable it gets when the temperature drops below freezing," Jess agreed readily, his grin reappearing. "No, there's no glitch. There was one in the beta version of the software—the prototype," he added in response to Del's frown and Susannah's blank look, "but it was ironed out long before we delivered. Saranno didn't know that, though. Like I say, he thought he was staring financial ruin in the face and he was desperate to avert it, but since he hadn't given the order to target Susannah, it wasn't his to rescind. All he could do was give me some information."

"Which you didn't trust," Tye said flatly.

"Which I wasn't a hundred percent sure of," Jess corrected him. "He confirmed Frank was in hock to his casino up to his eyeballs, and that it was apparent he was never going to be able to make good on his losses. He even let it slip that he'd considered sending an enforcer out to make an object lesson of Barrett. Except then he found out someone was going to save him the trouble."

"There was a contract out on Frank already," Tye said flatly. "Don't tell me—it was a prison hit, right?"

Jess stared at him. "You knew?" His tone took on a slight asperity. "So help me, Adams, if you let me go ahead and set up a meet with a wise guy when all the time you—"

"I didn't know," Tye said tonelessly. "But something in Susannah's statement to Sheriff Bannerman after the attack on her at Greta's place made me see it as a possibility, and I ran my own check on Frank. My methods weren't as cutting-edge as yours," he added with a shrug. "Just plain old-fashioned legwork by one of my operatives."

"What did I say?" Susannah folded her hands in her lap and looked inquiringly at Tye. He frowned.

"What?"

"What did I say?" she repeated. "You said something in my statement to the sheriff alerted you, Tye. I'm asking you what it was."

"Oh." He scrubbed his jaw with his hand. "It was that cornpone remark. You told Bannerman the shooter made some crack about the way you spoke, something about it being a while since he'd heard an accent like yours."

"I see." She remembered now, Susannah thought. She'd tried to put those horrifying moments in Greta's garage behind her, but in some buried corner of her mind she'd probably always be able to relive the fear she'd felt when she'd known her son was in danger. She tried to control the tremor in her voice. "And when were you planning to tell me you were following up on this clue?"

He looked disconcerted. "I didn't see the need to until I'd found out whether it meant anything or not."

He wouldn't, she thought, her brief anger edging into resignation. All his life Tye had been used to playing a lone hand, and if that was a natural result of growing up as the son of Marvin Adams she could see how he might not realize the rules had changed.

But they had. For her that change had come yesterday when she'd understood that he'd not only taken on the task of protecting her and Danny, but that he was fully prepared to give up his own life for theirs.

You didn't set a limit on your commitment to me, she thought, meeting his gaze across the table. *That's when I knew I didn't want to set a limit on my commitment to you.*

Her decision had led to the night they'd just spent in each other's arms—which brought her right back to the matter at hand.

Tye Adams was going to have to get used to the fact that she was part of his life now.

"I should have told you." As if his thoughts had been following the same course as hers, he exhaled sharply. "Dammit, Suze, I should have told you, of course. You've got a right to know what's going on."

"Yes, I do." She gave the words a significance he

couldn't miss. "What did your operative find out about Frank's time in prison?"

"That his last two weeks there were spent in the infirmary. Apparently during an exercise period in the yard, another inmate stuck a homemade shiv between Frank's ribs. It just missed his heart. But that's not all. Barrett was serving his time in your home state— a fact that I passed on to Bannerman when I spoke to him on the phone today."

Something else he hadn't told her about, Susannah thought tightly. But she couldn't worry about that right now. "West Virginia Penitentiary?"

"Mount Olive, although he started out in—" he began, but she didn't let him finish.

"What are you saying, Tye? My baby's not in danger because of who his daddy was, but because of his mama? That you think there's a *link* between me and these killers?"

This was why he hadn't wanted to tell her, she realized, nameless dread running through her. Part of his reluctance had been because he wasn't used to opening up to someone else, but part of it had been because he'd wanted to spare her for as long as he could. He'd learned something. Whatever it was, he was afraid it would tear her world apart.

"There is a link," he said flatly. "Maybe it's not relevant, maybe it's just a coincidence, but there is a link, Susannah. And what Bannerman told me when I called made me realize it's a stronger one than I thought. You ever hear of a little hamlet called Germantown Bend?"

"No." Her answer was automatic. She frowned, and qualified it. "I'm not sure. I think I remember the

Amish people we stayed with in Pennsylvania asking Granny Lacey if she knew anyone there. Where's Germantown Bend, and why is it important?''

"Germantown Bend's only thirty miles from another little hamlet—one called Fox Hollow," Tye said steadily. "It's probably not important at all, except that the prints from the shooter in Greta's garage came back to Bannerman today with an identification. His name was Waylon Lynds, Suze. And he was born and raised in Germantown Bend.''

"HOW ARE YOU holding up, sweetheart?'' Del directed a keen glance Susannah's way as he made his way stiffly down the porch steps beside her. She managed a smile.

"Like I just got kicked in the stomach by a bad-tempered old she-mule,'' she confessed, gently uncurling Danny's tugging fist from her hair. "Do you think there's any way Sheriff Bannerman's information could be wrong?''

Minutes after Tye's revelation Del had invited Susannah to walk over to the bunkhouse with him when he went to examine Kevin Bradley's horse. In a tone that had brooked no opposition he'd put Tye and Jess on KP duty, telling them to meet him at the bunkhouse corral when they were finished scrubbing pans.

Susannah had known the older man's maneuver had been for the sole purpose of giving her time to collect herself after the shock of Tye's news. From his quiet agreement she'd realized Tye had understood what was behind Del's suggestion, too.

"Hank Bannerman's no Columbo, and he goes off half-cocked sometimes.'' Del steadied himself with his cane as they crossed the gravel drive. He met her eyes. "Yeah, I heard his theory about Greta the next day when I stopped in at his office on my way back from the hospital. I tore one hell of a strip off him over it, but I think even by then he'd found he couldn't make it fit the facts."

"You love her, don't you?" Momentarily diverted from her own problems, Susannah waited for his reply. He looked away.

"More than I realized," he said shortly. "When I saw she'd been hit all I could think was that if she survived, I'd spend the rest of my life proving it to her."

He halted. "Funny how you find out what you really want when you nearly lose it, isn't it?" he said evenly.

From the first she'd felt as easy with this man as she would have with her own father, Susannah thought. She didn't pretend to misunderstand what had been behind his question.

"Is it that obvious?" She looked down, stirring a tuft of her son's hair with a gentle finger. "I spent the night with him, Del. He wants a future with me and Danny."

Gray eyes narrowed in the tanned face turned to her. "Does he, now?" He exhaled sharply, and then nodded. "Then I'm glad, sweetheart—for you and for that lucky son-of-a-gun. When's the happy day?"

"Oh, we won't make any plans until this business is all over with," she replied, slightly flustered. "Maybe I shouldn't even have told you, but—"

"I'll keep my big mouth shut and act surprised when he springs it on me," Del reassured her. "And if you're looking for an ex-Double B to escort you down the aisle when the time comes, I'd be glad to stand in for your father, Susannah.''

"I'd hoped you'd say that." She felt a stinging moisture behind her eyelids and blinked rapidly. "For heaven's sake, it seems like every time I turn around these days I'm tearing up," she said shakily.

"It's the stress." As they resumed walking, he frowned. "This Waylon Lynds—you sure you never heard of him before?"

Helplessly she shook her head. "Like I told Tye, Granny Lacey didn't stay in touch with anyone from Fox Hollow, let alone a town thirty miles away from it. She kept up correspondence with the Amish ladies we'd known, and the friends she made in the other places we'd lived, though," she added, her brow furrowing. "I never thought much about it before, but now I wonder why she didn't write home once in a while."

"Maybe after the tragedies that happened there your grandmother needed to put Fox Hollow behind her completely," Del replied quietly. "I can understand that." He fell silent for a moment, and then continued, his tone brisker. "Let's concentrate on what we do know. This Waylon Lynds was a bad egg and from what Bannerman was told by the West Virginia authorities, his twin brother Lyle wasn't any better—although apparently they were saints compared to some of their uncles and cousins. I think it's safe to assume Lyle was one of the two other shooters," he added. "Bannerman told Tye the Lynds brothers apparently worked as a team."

"Which leaves one unaccounted for, as Tye said."

Susannah bit her lip. "I've tried and tried, and I just can't come up with any reason why someone would want me dead, Del. Waylon Lynds said something about it being payback. That made some kind of sense when we thought I was only being targeted because of my connection with Frank, but if I'm the one they've always wanted—oh!"

Susannah felt the blood drain from her face as the full impact of what she'd just said hit her.

"Frank was murdered because of *me*," she whispered hoarsely. "If I'm linked to the killers somehow, then he was just as much an innocent bystander as Greta and Mr. Stephanopoulos."

"And you," Del said sharply. "Don't blame yourself for—" He stopped in midsentence, his jaw tightening. "What the hell does that damned fool think he's doing? He's got the animal on a slip-halter, for God's sake!"

Following his glance, she saw what he was talking about. Kevin Bradley, his face contorted in rage, was barely hanging on to the horse he was leading toward them. Even as she watched he wrenched viciously at the halter and the beast seemed to stumble.

With a scream of agony that set off an answering wail in a startled Danny, it lifted its back leg off the ground. The next moment Susannah saw the horse jerk its head upward, its eyes rolling in anguish, and the lead shank Bradley had been controlling it with whipped out of his hand to trail uselessly on the ground.

"Over there—the machine shed." Del raised his voice above Danny's frightened sobs. "Run to it as fast as you can, sweetheart. That animal's out of its mind with pain and it's heading this way.''

But already she'd seen the danger for herself. Rearing and whinnying frantically, the gelding suddenly broke into a flat-out gallop, its front hooves smashing down with such force into the packed dirt that when a horseshoe made contact with a stone Susannah's fearful gaze caught the flash of a spark. Desperately she began running toward the building Del had indicated, her arms wrapped tightly around Danny, adrenaline doubling her speed.

And still she wasn't going to be fast enough, she saw, cold fear coursing through her.

Del's disability was seldom allowed to curtail his activities, but in a situation like this there was no denying it held him back. As the animal had thundered by him he'd made a desperate attempt to catch the trailing end of its lead, but at the last minute it had changed course, veering out of his reach. Glancing over her shoulder as she ran, Susannah saw the pain-crazed gelding, its nostrils flared and ropes of foamy spittle swinging from its mouth, bearing down on her and her baby.

She did the only thing she could think of.

She let herself fall to her knees and then fully to the ground, her body curved protectively around Danny, who was now crying at the top of his lungs. Squeezing her eyes shut, she waited for the hammer-like hooves to come slicing down, her numb lips moving silently in prayer.

Take me, Lord, but please—save my little boy. Thy—Thy will be—

''Susannah!''

Incredulously she looked up, her eyes flying open in shock.

Tye was racing toward the runaway horse, and from the angle of his path it was obvious his intention wasn't to draw level with the animal.

He meant to cut directly across the path of nearly half a ton of dangerously out-of-control horseflesh, Susannah thought in terror.

Chapter Twelve

"Tye!"

As Susannah screamed out his name she saw him take one last, impossible leap. A split second later he was in front of those scything hooves.

"*No!*" The almost incoherent denial felt as if it was being ripped from her throat. She tried to scramble to her feet, but with both arms clasping her small son to her breast her balance was unsteady. A strong grip hauled her upright.

It was Jess, his face a grim mask, but even as he took her arm his features froze. Her own gaze widened in disbelief.

As the gelding's front legs came knifing down, Tye's leap became a paratrooper-like roll that took him just past those lethal hooves. He was back on his feet immediately, and grabbing for the trailing end of the lead.

His palms closed over it. The next moment he was jerked sideways as the gelding's momentum eliminated all slack in the rope. Half running, half dragged beside the animal, he didn't release his hold on the lead, and as his boots found purchase and his heels dug into the hard-packed dirt his efforts finally paid off.

The gelding's head snapped around as the halter lead tautened. Tye instantly took advantage of the situation, bearing down on the lead to prevent the big animal from rearing up.

As if some switch had been turned off in its brain, suddenly all fight seemed to go out of the horse. Flanks heaving, its shoulders trembling, it whickered once and then blew out its breath in a long, shuddering snuffle.

"Hero material," Jess said hoarsely from beside her. He shook his head. "Dammit, only Adams could pull off a stunt like that without killing himself. I thought for sure he was a goner."

"So did I." Her own voice was equally unsteady. "How did he—"

"Hold it right there, Bradley!"

The curt command came from Del, Susannah saw, but the man it was directed toward ignored it. Kevin Bradley, his face white with fury, strode up to within a few feet of Tye and the exhausted, trembling horse he was attempting to calm.

"Goddamn nag," the hired hand said thickly. "I knew a week after I bought it I'd end up selling its carcass for dogmeat. Stand out of the way, Adams."

He brought up a shaking hand. The revolver he was holding wavered, and then steadied.

"What nearly happened here was no one's fault but yours, Bradley." Tye's tone was ominously even. "You're not killing this animal to cover up your own criminal irresponsibility."

"You're also not staying on my land another minute.'' Leaning heavily on his cane, Del confronted the man. "I'll give you two weeks wages in lieu of notice, and whatever you paid for this horse, Kevin," he said quietly. "I just want you gone. Understand?"

It seemed his ex-employee did, Susannah thought with relief as Bradley slowly lowered his weapon. Shooting a look of impotent dislike at all three men, he turned on his heel and headed for the bunkhouse.

"Jess, you want to take over from here?" Tye's voice was husky. "I better take a look at this shoulder of mine. Feels like I might have busted open a couple of stitches."

As Jess readily took the lead from him and coaxed the now-docile and limping animal toward its corral, Tye one-handedly unbuttoned his shirt and began shrugging his left arm out of its blood-soaked sleeve. Susannah bit back a gasp and stepped forward.

"Heavens, Tye—that's not from a few opened stitches! One of his hooves must have just missed crushing your arm!" She peered worriedly at the raw gash slicing across the original wound. "You're going to have to have that looked at by a doctor. It could get infected."

"Susannah's right," Del interjected before Tye could voice a protest. "I'm taking you in to Last Chance to see Doc Jennings right now. You're going to need a tetanus shot, for starters."

"In the morning," Tye argued. "For God's sake, I'm not going to get lockjaw overnight, Del, and I'm not leaving Susannah and Danny here unprotected."

"Thanks for the vote of confidence, buddy." Jess rejoined them, his expression uncharacteristically somber as he took in Tye's injury. "I don't see why

Johnson and I can't keep a lid on things here until you and Del return. You're not going to be much use to anyone if you end up in hospital with blood poisoning.''

''Please, Tye.'' Susannah looked down at a red-faced and tear-streaked Danny, whose sobs had trailed off into a steady grizzling. ''Hush, starshine,'' she said softly, dropping a kiss on the downy head. ''It's all over now. Tye saved us.''

She looked back up at Tye. ''You did save us. Again,'' she added quietly. Her eyes met his, and for a moment it was as if there was no one but her and her baby and the man she loved. Then she took a deep breath and affixed a quelling frown to her features.

''You might be a hero like Jess says, Tyler Adams. But you've got to be the most pig-headed, stubborn, *exasperating* hero the Double B ever produced. The ranch won't fall apart because you're gone a couple of hours. *I* won't fall apart. And there's another thing I don't think you men have thought of.''

Del nodded. ''You mean that if Bradley sees us going into Last Chance he'll think twice about stopping there himself, and shooting off his mouth over a few beers at the local bar?'' He looked at Tye. ''You know the old phrase, 'head him off at the pass?' It might be a good idea to do some heading off with Kevin, before he tells all and sundry how ticked he was about guarding a woman and a baby on the Double B.''

IT WAS ONLY that last that had convinced Tye, Susannah thought an hour later as she unlatched a sleepy Danny from her breast and rose to put him in his crib.

Buttoning the bodice of her dress and stepping quietly from the room, she wandered into the kitchen, feeling oddly out of sorts and not knowing why.

Oh, you do so know why, Susannah Bird, she chided herself mentally. *It's because you feel like you're only half alive when he's not around. It's because you want him in your arms, want to have him wrapping his arms around you, want to hear him say again that he loves you and that he wants to marry you.*

Had he actually used those words? The question dropped, uninvited and unwelcome, into her mind. Frowning, she filled the cast-iron kettle and set it on the cookstove, but before she could continue her train of thought a soft knock came at the screen door a few feet away.

"Miz Barrett?" Paul Johnson touched the brim of his hat and opened the door. His glance took in the kettle she'd just set to boil. "If that's tea you're making I wouldn't say no to a cup myself," he said, keeping his tone low. "Is your little mister asleep?"

"I just put him down." Susannah smiled. "You're welcome to sit and have a cup of tea with me, Mr. Johnson. Pull out a chair while the kettle boils."

He shook his head firmly. "I wouldn't feel easy leaving my post for that long, ma'am. I'll do another perimeter check of the house and then have mine on the porch, if you don't mind. It's a whole lot more comfortable than sitting in the dark guarding the access gate like Mr. Crawford is right now, at that." He gave one of his rare grins. "I just wanted to step in and thank you for the plate of supper you kept warm for me."

"I only wish you could have gotten it inside you

sooner,'' Susannah said regretfully. ''Your ex-partner wasn't the greatest company at the table, but I guess we won't have to worry about him anymore.''

When Johnson had shown up after Del and Tye's departure, he'd told her Del had informed him of Kevin Bradley's altered status when he'd stopped at the perimeter gate on his way to Doc Jennings's clinic with Tye. He'd known something was up when Kevin had driven by a few minutes earlier like a bat out of hell, without a nod or a lifted hand.

On Del's instructions, Paul had left his post at the gate and Jess had taken over from him—mainly, Susannah suspected, because Del had wanted to give the hired hand a chance to have a hot meal and because the ex-marine knew that even the most alert soldier could get fatigued without a change of scenery once in a while.

''I feel bad I didn't get on his case harder over that horse,'' Johnson said with a grimace. ''He didn't like folks poking into his business so I didn't make a point of looking the animal over myself. I should have.''

''I know Del blames himself, too.'' Susannah shook her head. ''Like Tye said, it's no one's fault but Bradley's, and it's not as if there hasn't been a lot else occupying everybody's mind lately. Thank goodness the veterinarian seems to feel the poor thing's going to pull through all right with the antibiotics he prescribed.''

How could two men be so different? she asked herself as, with another brief touch to the brim of his hat, Johnson left to reassure himself all was secure outside. *As Granny Lacey would say, it takes all kinds,* she decided, dropping a couple of tea bags into a thick china teapot. A tiny bell rang faintly in her mind at the random thought, and she wrinkled her brow in an effort to pinpoint what it was that had just rippled across her subconscious.

Did the police ever catch the hit-and-run driver who killed her?

In the act of lifting the steaming kettle from the stove, Susannah froze. Slowly she set it down off the flame. Like an automaton she slid her hand into an oven mitt, picked up the cast-iron lifter and inserted it into the heavy metal cover, replacing the cover over the open hole in the stove's surface. The red flicker of the fire beneath disappeared from view. Walking over to the table on legs that felt suddenly weak, she sat down, her thoughts racing.

It had seemed outlandishly far-fetched when Tye had half suggested it a few days ago. But that had been when they'd still thought the killers who had been tracking her were connected in some way to Frank.

"Except they weren't," she said out loud. "They're connected to Fox Hollow. And that means there was a connection to Granny Lacey, too. Dear Lord—what if it *wasn't* just a tragic accident? What if she was murdered?"

Nausea rose in her throat, and she gripped the sturdy wooden edge of the table so tightly that her knuckles whitened. After a moment the sick dizziness passed and slowly she got to her feet again.

Tye had likely come to the same conclusion, she realized. If he had, he'd probably alerted the Atlantic City police to reopen the file on the unsolved hit-and-run. Although just hours earlier she'd tartly informed him that she didn't want to be left out of any part of this investigation, she didn't really regret he hadn't told her, she admitted unhappily.

Alice Tahe believed in an evil that walked like a man, talked like a man, looked like a man when it chose to. Whether that stalking evil went by the name of Skinwalker or not, the old lady was right, Susannah thought. Lacey Bird had lived her life serving her God and bringing new life safely into the world, and something evil had brutally struck her down before her time.

She squeezed her eyes shut to hold back the tears. Almost immediately they flew open again.

From somewhere outside had come the sound of a heavy thump, as if a dead weight had fallen onto the porch. Even as Susannah froze into stillness all the lights, including the ones illuminating the yard, went out.

The tiny hairs on the back of her neck rose. Every nerve ending in her body seemed to be on instant full alert, straining to bring in whatever information—a sound, a scent, anything at all—might mean the difference between survival and death. She had no doubt at all that there was someone out there who wanted to kill her, and she was almost positive that the thump she'd heard had been Paul's body hitting the porch.

One by one, every defense had somehow been breached—she wouldn't let herself wonder what had happened to Jess—and now all that stood between the evil outside and the innocently sleeping infant in the room just down the hall was her. For a moment a sense of hopelessness overwhelmed her, and she had the childish impulse to run into her bedroom, lock the door behind her, and huddle with Danny in the clothes closet until Tye and Del returned.

And if they don't return in time? she asked herself coldly. *Is that how you want to die, Susannah Bird—like a rat hiding in the dark, hoping you won't be found? Is that how you want to let your baby die—in the arms of a mother who was too frightened to stand and fight for him?*

There were guns in the cupboard by the screen door. They might as well have been on the moon, since she didn't have the key to open it, and only this morning she'd asked Del to lock her own revolver in with the rest of the weapons for safety's sake. Briefly Susannah considered edging over to the counter for one of the knives in the knife block sitting there, and just as quickly discarded the option. She could handle a gun, she told herself. She wouldn't have the first idea of how to use a knife against an opponent, and the odds were good that the weapon would end up being turned against her.

Which left…what? What could she use, not only for defense but to attack if she had to?

Quietly she moved to the cookstove. On the counter beside it was the padded oven mitt and the cast-iron lifter—it looked like a bent handle—which, when inserted into a slot on one of the heavy metal disks covering the round holes in the top of the stove, was used to lift the hot covers safely. She did exactly that.

The man stalking her could be anywhere, and the longer she stayed here the longer he had that advantage over her. She needed him to be unsure of her whereabouts, too. Cautiously she pushed open the screen door and slipped out onto the porch.

Her back to the wall of the house, swiftly she moved a few feet farther down the length of the porch. She paused, straining her ears for any hint of a sound, straining her eyes for the slightest shadowy movement.

Nothing. She took another step.

The next moment she was backing up frantically, shock washing over her in waves, her legs and arms feeling clumsy and in the way. Her balance wildly off-kilter, she grabbed desperately with her free hand for something to steady herself, and her reaching fingers clamped onto a familiar surface.

For a long moment she just stood there, holding on to the back of one of the sturdy porch chairs and willing her heart to stop crashing against her ribs.

She'd stepped on a body—or more exactly, a hand. She was pretty sure, Susannah thought disjointedly, that she'd just stepped on Paul Johnson's hand. But she had to make certain. And that meant she had to go back to that lifeless form.

It was Johnson. On her knees beside him a second later, first she recognized the feel of the oiled denim work jacket he'd been wearing when he'd spoken with her in the kitchen less than half an hour ago, and then her searching fingers brushed against the woven horse-hair band she'd noticed he always wore around his left wrist. She sat back on her heels, fighting back grief and despair.

This can't be right, Lord, she thought numbly. *The good ones keep dying and getting hurt. Maybe Granny Lacey could make some sense of this—likely her faith would be so strong she wouldn't even need for it to make sense—but it seems all wrong to me.*

"It *is* all wrong," she whispered. She picked up the stove plate in her mittened hand and slowly she stood, rising to her full height. Only then did she realize she'd been creeping along in a half crouch before. Her grip on the cast-iron lifter tightened.

"And You're going to use me to put it right, aren't You?" she whispered huskily. "Sorry, Lord. I should have figured it out sooner."

She was a new mama girded with an oven mitt and armed with part of a cookstove. He was a killer, and since he'd used firearms before, she assumed he had one now. One of them was going to walk away from this and one of them wasn't, and the odds were unfairly stacked.

Against him, Susannah thought calmly. He didn't know that yet. Soon he would.

"My granny used to say the only thing worse'n a live skunk hanging around under the front stoop and stinkin' up the night air was a dead one," she said loudly. "I figure in a few minutes you're going to be dead vermin, mister. Why don't you come out into the open so I don't have to worry about dragging you out from your hidey hole later on?"

"You know, lady, it doesn't worry me a whole lot, being compared to a skunk." From the other end of the porch the shadows gathered and became the shape of a man. He walked toward her, his pace unhurried. "They stick to their own kind, and they don't really give a damn if the rest of the world don't like them. But you—"

He stopped about five feet away from her, and although she couldn't make out his features she knew he was smiling.

"You're like a little mama rabbit. Just couldn't resist comin' out of your warm, safe nest and seeing what was going on. I used to catch 'em like that. Jiggle a piece of string outside of a rabbit hole and wait till one got curious."

She saw the white glimmer of a cast on his right arm, and knew she was looking at the results of Tye's shooting three nights ago. He took another step.

"Uh-huh. Those little rabbits, seems like they purely couldn't help themselves. Just like you won't be able to."

"You're Lyle Lynds, aren't you?" Susannah heard the tremor in her voice, and instantly stilled it. "I saw your brother Waylon die. He wanted to kill me, too."

She'd hoped to throw him off balance. She realized too late that instead she'd brought his anger from lazy malevolence to sharp focus.

"Right from the start I couldn't credit how much damn grief you gave us," he said, anger edging his tone. "Now my brother's dead because of you and that brat of yours."

"Your brother's dead because he was holding a gun on me and my baby," she retorted. "Why did Mr. Stephanopoulos have to die? Why did Paul Johnson have to, and for all I know, Jess Crawford?"

"Crawford's the one at the gate?" Lynds gave a snort. "I wouldn't want you to leave this old world worryin' your pretty head about something you don't need to. He was occupied with a diversion when I snuck onto the property, so I didn't see any reason to kill him."

"Thank God," Susannah said softly. Surreptitiously she shifted her weight onto the balls of her feet. ''But there's still been too many deaths. I intend to put an end to them right now, mister.''

Even before she'd finished speaking she lunged at him, bringing the thick iron plate around in a swinging arc aimed at his head. He moved almost as quickly. She saw his right hand move clumsily toward the opened front of his jacket, saw him realize his mistake, saw him start to reach for what she guessed was a shoulder-holstered gun with his left hand.

The still-hot iron plate struck him lower than she'd meant, connecting so solidly with the side of his jaw that she felt the jarring impact running down into her shoulder socket like a numbing jolt of electricity. His head snapped sideways and again he forgot his injured arm. Involuntarily, both of his hands flew to his face and a curious, high-pitched whistling noise came from his wide-open mouth.

She'd left something on the cookstove, Susannah thought in sudden fear. It had started to burn—she could *smell* it.

She could smell seared flesh and hair…his flesh and hair, she realized a heartbeat later. She'd burned him. She'd caused him excruciating pain, because that whistling noise was the sound of a man trying to draw enough breath into his lungs to scream, and she'd probably branded him for life. But none of that was good enough, because she hadn't killed him.

She'd known one of them would walk away from this. She'd known one of them wouldn't. She saw Lynds's left hand fumble in his jacket, and then she saw the gun he was pointing at her, heard the explosion.

Even in what little light there was she could make

out the expression of total disbelief that crossed his features. And even in the near dark it was impossible to miss the neat, round hole that had suddenly bloomed in the middle of his forehead.

He fell lifelessly to the floor of the porch, his gun dropping from his limp fingers and skidding across the wooden boards. Even as Susannah turned shakily around, the lights of a vehicle being driven too fast into the yard illuminated the man standing behind her, his just-fired gun still in his hand.

Paul Johnson swayed on his feet and then steadied himself.

"That tea," he said thickly. "I b'lieve I'll take it sitting down at the kitchen table after all, Miz Barrett."

Chapter Thirteen

"They say it never rains there, starshine."

Leaning back in one of the comfortably cushioned porch chairs, Susannah lifted her face to the warmth of the midmorning sun. In her arms, Danny made an impatient movement, and contritely she switched her attention back to him.

"No, I'm not fibbing, little man. No rain, oranges growing in your backyard, and movie stars so thick on the ground a body pretty near trips over them every time she goes out for a quart of milk. What do you say? D'you think you'd like being a California baby?"

In answer, Danny reached up and grabbed on to a strand of her hair. He gave it an interested tug, and she winced.

"I'll take that as a yes," she said, retrieving her hair.

Del had said this part of the porch was his favorite, Susannah mused, and she was inclined to agree. From here it was impossible to see the place where Lyle Lynds had died last night, although when she'd stepped out of the kitchen door onto the porch she'd had to walk around the thoroughly scrubbed and still-damp patch where his body had lain until Sheriff Bannerman had ordered it removed.

"Tye not back yet?" Dropping a battered leather duffel bag on the porch floor, Jess sat down in the chair beside her and gave an enormous yawn. He grinned unrepentantly at her.

"I'll be glad to get back to the city, where folks go to bed at a decent hour," he said wryly. "I got four hours of shut-eye. How about you?"

"Total exhaustion did the trick for me," Susannah confessed. "I think my mind just decided to blank out everything that had happened for a few hours."

"I wish I could have done that. Hell, I'm still going over it, wondering how I could have screwed up so badly." Jess's tone was uncharacteristically harsh. "If that bastard Lynds had brought his gun butt down half an inch either way, Johnson might have ended up with a whole lot worse than the mother of all headaches. And you and Danny might have ended up——" Savagely he rubbed his palm across his mouth, not finishing his sentence.

"You didn't screw up," she protested swiftly. "No one expected Kevin Bradley to pull off onto that side road and wait until Del and Tye had gone before returning to the ranch. Who knows what he was planning to do if you hadn't stopped him from coming back onto the property?"

She bit her lip thoughtfully. "He never did show up in Last Chance last night, so Del's hopeful he's well out of the county by now. But wherever he is, he's gone, Lyle Lynds is dead, and Danny and I are fine."

"Thanks to Johnson." A ghost of Jess's familiar grin touched his features. "Would you believe he's out with a post-hole digger right now, setting some new fence in the west quarter? He told Del he didn't figure a little thing like a bump on the head should keep a man from doing an honest day's work."

"When I tried to thank him last night he didn't want to hear it," Susannah nodded. "He said he'd been the rankest kind of greenhorn, letting himself get bushwacked by Lynds, and if he'd stayed out of the fight a couple more seconds he had no doubt I would have finished Lyle off by myself."

She smiled, but then her smile faded. "That's not true," she said softly. "I think Lynds might have gotten off that shot he was trying for before Paul could stop him if he'd had the use of his gun hand. I've got Tye to thank for that."

"Speak of the devil and he shall appear," Jess said lightly, squinting at the access road leading to the Double B, where a cloud of dust was rapidly approaching. "He did that on purpose," he added, a note of wicked humor in his voice.

"Did what?" Susannah shielded her eyes with one hand, her heart leaping the way it did every time Tye came into sight. It probably always would leap, she thought helplessly.

"Rode the Harley into Last Chance for his meeting with Bannerman," Jess said as the motorcycle made a curving swoop that brought it to a standstill beside Del's pickup. "He knew that would chap the sherf's butt."

A gurgle of laughter escaped her and in her arms Danny gurgled, too, as if he appreciated Jess's fool-

ishness as much as she did. Maybe she had no right
to laugh yet, she told herself as she heard the screen
door slam and the sound of Del's cane joining Tye's
booted footsteps, but on a God-given day like this
laughter seemed just one more precious gift.

And instead of focusing on the horrors of the previous night, she preferred instead to recall the way Tye
had vaulted over the porch railing and gathered her to
him as he and Del had arrived just in time to see the
shot that had taken Lynds down. He'd held her so
tightly it had seemed as if he never wanted to let her
go, Susannah remembered. It was only when the porch
lights had suddenly gone on—she'd learned later that
Del had reset the outside breaker that Lynds had obviously turned off—that he'd finally released her
enough to gaze into her face. She'd seen the raw fear
in those blue eyes, seen the harshly carved lines bracketing his mouth.

"I thought I'd lost you." His whisper had been
hoarse. "Dear God, Susannah—I thought I'd *lost*
you."

After the authorities had finally packed up and left
and a weary-looking Del had announced his intention
of trying to get some sleep before rising for morning
chores, Tye had made no attempt to conceal the fact
that he was spending the night in her room. During
the too-few hours remaining before dawn she'd
drowsily opened her eyes once or twice. Each time
she had she'd realized that the man cradling her in his
arms was wide awake and watching over her. When
the first pink streaks of morning were painting the sky
she'd awakened to find him on the edge of the bed,

wearing a pair of jeans and nothing else and talking in a low tone into his cell phone.

"I owe you one, Virge." He'd seen her sleepily rub her eyes, and immediately his free hand had reached for one of hers. "Yeah, Bannerman and I seemed to have worked out our past differences. He phoned me half an hour ago, asked me if I could pull some strings and get the identification process fast-tracked."

He'd fallen silent for a moment, and she'd seen his expression relax slightly. He'd nodded. "It'll be good to see you again, too, buddy. Jess was saying the other day that us Double B's should have kept in touch more closely, and he's right. Del hasn't heard from Gabe yet, but that's not surprising."

He'd rung off and turned to her with an apologetic smile. "Virgil Connor's off assignment and I asked him to get the FBI to look into something for me. This isn't the way I planned on waking you up, honey."

He'd grimaced. "I hadn't planned on taking off right away, either, but Bannerman says one of his deputies called in a report of a burned-out vehicle being found in a nearby canyon. There was a body in it, and although it's going to take a forensics team to confirm identification, this time I think we caught a break."

Something in his cautiously optimistic tone had alerted her. She'd scooted bolt upright in the bed, and only when she'd seen the heat flare in his gaze did she realize the demurely buttoned front of her cotton nightie was no longer demure, was, in fact, barely buttoned. Flushing, she'd drawn the two edges of the garment together. He'd smiled wryly.

He'd pulled her to him, kissed her hard on her lips,

and released her. "That was to tide me over," he'd said softly.

He'd inhaled and raked his hand through his hair with a quick frown. "A certain Jasper Scudder served time in Mount Olive Correctional with Frank. Scudder was Waylon and Lyle's cousin. And his driver's license was found in a wallet a few feet away from that burnt-out wreck with the body in it."

She hadn't let herself hope too much, Susannah thought now as Del and Tye joined her and Jess. But judging from the quick wink Del shot her as he sat down, it seemed as if Tye's news was good.

It was. It was also unsettling.

"Virgil Connor's on his way here, but he called me at Bannerman's office. All preliminary findings seem to confirm that the body from the burned car is Scudder's," he said without preamble, as if he didn't want to keep her in suspense any longer than necessary. "Apparently he broke his right leg years ago in prison, and the body's skeleton shows an old break in that leg. The DNA results will clinch things when they come in, but there really wasn't a lot of doubt in the first place."

"He was the marksman who shot at the two of you on the *Dinetah*," Del said slowly. "He would have had to be. Lyle fumbled drawing his gun with his left hand last night, so he couldn't have managed any kind of sharpshooting the day before."

"That's what Bannerman and Matt Tahe figure. The Tribal Police were informed because of the likelihood that the person who tried to kill us on their land was one and the same as the body in the car. The theory is that the accident that killed him occurred

shortly after he left the scene the day before yesterday.''

"So, it's over?'' Susannah's voice shook with emotion. "After all these months it's really over, Tye?''

His gaze met hers. "It's really over, Suze. You can
begin to live a normal life again,'' he said quietly.

"Thank God,'' she breathed, tightening her hold on
Danny and closing her suddenly tear-filled eyes. She
opened them again at his next words.

"We still don't know why he was targeting you,
honey. Now that the Bureau's involved, Connor says
the FBI wants to interview you to see if there's any
connection we've overlooked. They're already in the
process of pulling not only Scudder's prison file but
his complete criminal record and the transcripts of his
parole hearings.''

She stared at him, confused. "But you said he was
in prison with Frank. That's the connection, Tye. We
were right the first time—I wasn't the link to the killers, Frank was. It's obvious he and this Scudder person had a falling out of some kind when they were in
the penitentiary together. Killing Frank's wife and
child was payback, like Waylon Lynds said.''

He'd been standing a few feet away from her. Now
he swiftly crossed to where she was sitting, hunkering
down beside her chair.

"I wish that were so, Suze,'' he said softly. "But
the time line's wrong. Scudder was released a month
or so before Frank's sentence was up. The Atlantic
City police confirmed only an hour ago that the
driver's license found by that body this morning was
the same one produced by the person who rented the

car that killed your grandmother. Scudder was after your family before you even met Frank.''

Beside her, Jess had been silent. Now he spoke. ''I thought Susannah said they'd closed the file on her grandmother's death.''

''They had.'' Tye nodded. ''I asked them to reopen it the day after the incident at Greta's. I was lucky enough to be put through to the detective who'd originally worked the case, and he admitted he'd never been happy about having to shelve the file. I think he was glad of the excuse to look into it one more time.''

Susannah wasn't listening. ''But none of this makes any *sense!*'' Even to her own ears her voice sounded thin and high. ''I've never heard the name Jasper Scudder until today. How did he know me? How did he know Granny Lacey? For heaven's sakes, the man had to have had some reason to want us dead, and there wasn't one! You just said Danny and I could live normally from now on, Tye, but what if Scudder has more relatives out there?''

''If he did, sweetheart, wouldn't it have been logical for them to have been with Lyle last night?'' Del's tone was soothing, his words reasonable, and something in Susannah snapped. She got to her feet. When Tye stood, too, she moved away from him to confront all three men.

''I guess that *is* the logical way to look at it,'' she said tightly. ''But I'm a mother now, and if I'm supposed to choose between logical and a mother's intuition, I'm going with the second one. Danny's not safe yet. He might *never* be safe. What kind of a birthright is that to pass on to my little boy?''

"I can understand how frustrating this has to be for you, Suze." Tye moved toward her. "But—"

"Birthright?" Del's interjection was sharp. "Wait a minute. Tye, did Bannerman mention what the date of birth was on Scudder's license?"

Tye shrugged. "I think he did, but I'd have to phone him to tell you what it was for sure." There was a touch of impatience in his answer. "Why is that important?"

"Maybe it's not," Del said slowly. "But maybe it's the one thing we've been overlooking all along. Just tell me—was he around your age or mine?"

"Yours. Maybe even a year or two older," Tye said shortly. "I still don't see what his age has to do with any—"

"Like I said, maybe it doesn't mean a thing."

Del passed a hand over his face. To her astonishment, Susannah saw a tremor run through him, and her anger vanished. In confusion she glanced at Tye and then Jess, but both men wore identically blank looks.

"Something came in the mail today." Del reached for his cane. "With all that's been going on, I didn't see the need to lay this particular puzzle out on the table for the rest of you. I thought it was meant only for me, although I'm damned if I can figure it out. Now I wonder if it's somehow tied in with everything else."

As he got to his feet he looked past the three of them, his gray eyes narrowing. Following his glance, Susannah saw another dust cloud roiling its way along the access road, although this one was approaching at a more sedate speed than Tye's Harley had.

"It's the Effa-Bee-Eye," Jess said laconically. "Now that it's all over bar the shouting, Virge shows up." He caught Susannah's eye and shrugged sheepishly. "Connor's a good guy, but he and I always seemed to rub each other the wrong way."

"That's because you were always jerking his chain," Del said with a return of his normally dry manner. A corner of his mouth lifted, but Susannah saw that the shadows remained in his eyes. "I'm glad he's here. Maybe he can help make sense of this. I'll be back in a second."

"Hell, I guess I should bury the hatchet, at that," Jess said with a grimace. He picked up the duffel bag at his feet. "I'll go throw this in the back of my car, and do the manly handshake thing with Mr. Straight Arrow."

"Those two were always getting into it with each other," Tye said as, with a martyred air, Jess disappeared around the corner of the porch. "But when a few Last Chance toughs ganged up on Jess once, Virge showed up and single-handedly took on the whole lot of them. He'd been sent to the Double B for street fighting and the local boys didn't stand a chance." He shrugged. "Virge would prefer to forget those days. Like Jess says, he's Mr. Straight Arrow now."

He turned to her, his expression softening. "Jess is leaving today. We could, too—you, me and Dan the Man. What do you say, Suze?"

"Leave for California?" She blinked, taken unawares by the suddenness of his suggestion. "Today?"

"Why not?" As if it was the most natural thing in

the world, casually he took Danny from her, holding his small namesake easily in one arm. With his other hand, gently he tipped her chin up.

"I don't blame you for not feeling completely safe yet, honey. You've been on the run for so long it's going to take a while for you to realize it's all over. I've got state-of-the-art security systems in the Malibu beach house and the Beverly Hills place, plus I can assign trained professionals to watch over you on a twenty-four/seven basis when I'm not around. If the FBI want to talk to you, they can do it there. Give me the word and I'll book us on the next flight out of Gallup."

She'd told him once that when she looked at him, she wanted to be different. He'd told her the same, Susannah thought, meeting that heaven-blue gaze and feeling the tears welling up behind her own eyes. They'd both been so wrong. He loved her for who she was, and she—

Oh, admit it, she told herself happily. *You gave him your heart the first day you met. Angel or devil, you handed it over to him without a second thought, and you knew even then you'd never be able to get it back.*

Her tears spilled over, but a joyful little bubble of laughter rose in her throat. "Yes," she said simply. "Oh, *yes,* Tye. Let's start our new life today."

"I was hoping you'd say that." He brought his mouth to hers, gently brushing a kiss against her lips. "Maybe this letter Del mentioned will unlock the whole mystery of why Scudder bore a grudge against you, Suze. Maybe the FBI will come up with the answer one of these days. But you're right—from now on we're going to put the past behind us and make our own life.''

"We'll have to tell Del to book a flight, too,'' she said, blushing slightly. "Oh, not until Greta's out of the hospital, of course. If he's going to give me away, I want her to be my matron of honor. Do you think it would be wrong for me to wear a real wedding dress, Tye?'' she said, sudden doubt assailing her. "I know I've been married before, and of course Danny's going to be there to see his mama get hitched, but I'd love to have the kind of dress I used to dream about when I was a little girl. Lace,'' she added dreamily. "Enough lace to choke a billy goat, and satin shoes that I'll never be able to use again.''

"You want Del to give you away?'' There was an odd note in Tye's voice, and she looked up at him, a little confused.

"I wish my own daddy was alive to walk his daughter down the aisle, Tye, just like I wish my mama was here.'' Her smile wavered. "But Del and he were as close as brothers once, so I figure some part of him will be there on my wedding day.''

"Suze, I don't think you under—'' Tye broke off as Jess rounded the corner of the porch. Accompanying him was a dark-haired man, wearing a suit and a tie and a ticked-off expression.

It looked as if Virgil Connor and Jess Crawford had already butted heads, Susannah thought. Her amusement was overlaid with a touch of frustration that they'd shown up just when they had, although she was pretty sure she knew what Tye had been about to say. She *did* understand, she told him silently as she watched him shift Danny's weight slightly in his arms and grip Virgil's outstretched hand with real affection.

They would be living together as husband and wife. Waiting for Del and Greta to be able to attend their wedding would mean it would be that much longer before their status was formalized, not only in the eyes of the law, but according to her most basic beliefs.

Granny Lacey wouldn't approve, she thought guiltily. A few weeks ago, she herself would never have believed she was capable of taking such a step. But that had been before she'd met the only man she would ever love.

It might be as long as a month before their marriage was blessed by a preacher, but it was important to her to have Del give her away, she thought. Tye would understand once she explained how she felt.

With a start, she realized she'd just been introduced to Virgil Connor and the dark-haired man was regarding her with a bemused expression. Hastily she stuck out her hand and shook the one he was proffering to her, just as Del appeared once more.

"I—I've heard all about you," she said shyly, and under straight brows Connor's green eyes widened briefly.

"All good, I hope?" he said politely.

"Pretty much all bad," she answered with raw honesty.

His laugh was startled, but genuinely amused. "So Tyler finally got himself a plain-speaking woman," he said with more warmth than he'd previously shown. "I always told him he needed a good dose of reality to keep himself balanced out there in La-La Land. This is your little boy?"

For the next few minutes Danny was duly admired. He didn't take it in stride. Even as they all began to sit down, Susannah's nose caught an unmistakable whiff. By the time she returned with a freshly diapered Danny, it was obvious from the conversation that Connor had been filled in on those details he hadn't previously been aware of.

"I'm with Tye, Del," he said with a frown. "What's the relevance of Jasper Scudder's age?"

"He's the right age, that's why it's relevant." Del reached into the snap-fastened breast pocket of his Western-style shirt, and pulled out what looked to Susannah's puzzled gaze like a postcard. His features tightened. "He's the right age to have served in 'Nam," he added hoarsely. "Take a look at this."

It was a postcard. Since she was sitting next to Del, Susannah was the first one he passed it to, and the photo on the front, as garishly overcolored and unreal as it was, evoked the same instant response in her that she'd experienced when she'd inhaled the perfume Tye had given her.

The Beautiful Blue Ridge Mountains, West Virginia, ran the caption. She looked up at Del, and the lines in his face relaxed for a moment.

"That's right, sweetheart." He nodded. "Your home state. But turn it over."

She did as he said. Her gaze flew back to his in shock. "I don't understand," she said, her voice uneven. "That—that's the symbol of the Double B's, Del. And those words written underneath—what do they mean? Who sent you this?"

"Maybe Jasper Scudder," he said heavily.

Distractedly she passed the card, with its crudely

drawn picture of two bees fighting to the death and its scrawled message—"Does this still mean something to you?"—to Tye, and saw Jess and Connor draw in closer to study it with him.

"And maybe it wasn't meant for me at all," Del continued. He met her eyes. His own were bleak.

"I think it was meant for Daniel Bird's daughter," he said softly.

Chapter Fourteen

"That's why it's a West Virginia postcard, instead of New Mexico or Texas or any other state," Del went on. "I wish I could make out the postmark, but it's practically invisible."

"The Bureau labs can bring that up to legibility," Connor said crisply. "Hold it by the edges, Jess. Even if the sender didn't use gloves his prints have probably been overlaid with those of a dozen or so postal employees, but we might as well be careful."

"Something happened over there all those years ago, didn't it?" Tye's question was quiet, but at it Susannah saw Del's strong hands clench. "Something so terrible the four of you original Double B's never spoke of it to anyone, am I right? And whatever it was, you think it came back to target Susannah for some reason." His last sentence wasn't a question, it was an accusation. Del's head jerked up:

"I don't know, dammit!" His tone was raw. "Scudder's dead, so even if my worst fears are right he's no longer a threat. But if I thought that anything I did—anything the four of us did over there—had put

Susannah through the hell she's endured these past nine months I'd never forgive—''

''If I thought that I'd find it damn hard to forgive you, too,'' Tye said tonelessly. ''Especially if by telling me sooner you could have prevented what almost happened last night.''

''There isn't anything to forgive.'' Susannah spoke loudly enough to ensure she had everyone's attention. She went on in the same tone, her voice steady. ''Those boys didn't ask to be sent over there. A whole bunch of them never came back, and those that did sure didn't get no hero's welcome, from what I hear. Now they've got a wall in Washington, D.C., and Greta told me there's another memorial right here in New Mexico, built by a daddy who lost his son in that war no one wanted to remember.''

''Angel Fire. Near the Taos Reservation,'' Jess murmured, looking down at his hands.

''That's right, in Angel Fire,'' she agreed. She met Del's anguished gaze. ''A couple of memorials. Some movies with pretty actors I figure don't come close to telling it like it was. Bracelets like the one you told us about, Del, with the names of young men, some of them never ever accounted for, put away in drawers near thirty years ago and long forgotten.'' She took a deep breath. ''I wonder how you can forgive *us*,'' she said softly. ''Whatever happened over there, I know you would have always tried to do the right thing, Del. I know my daddy would have, too.''

''We tried. I'm not sure we succeeded in the end.'' His voice was barely audible. ''Beta Beta Force was only as honorable as the four men in it, and one of them never should have been a soldier, let alone a member of a covert operations group.''

''MacLeish?'' Jess said. ''The one who killed his wife and then himself?''

Del looked up in faint surprise. ''Not John, no. Zeke Harmon.''

''You said he died over there,'' Susannah said, confused. Del nodded.

''His remains were found and identified. That was after he rigged the bomb that left me like this.''

He made an impatient gesture toward his stiffly splayed-out legs—his prosthetic legs. He went on, his tone low, and she realized he wasn't just retelling the past, he was reliving it.

''Our jobs weren't pretty and there wasn't a rule book, but like you said, we tried to remember we were men, not beasts. At some point Zeke must have forgotten that. Stories began to circulate about a rogue killer who didn't care who he targeted—soldiers, civilians, the enemy, American boys. Beta Beta was assigned to find the killer and bring him in.''

''And eventually you discovered he was right there, hiding in plain sight?'' Connor asked. ''One of the Double B's?''

''Eventually.'' Del passed a hand across his eyes. ''We probably should have figured it out sooner, but he was one of us, dammit. Zeke had saved my life more than once, and I'd saved his. He and John were best buddies. So maybe we bore some responsibility for the last few murders he committed before we arrested him. I know when it all came out afterward more than a few who'd lost friends figured we'd been part of a cover-up. I was told there'd been threats made against the remaining Double B's lives.''

"And you think Scudder might have been one of those who wanted revenge. He looked up my daddy, found he was dead, and went after me and the people I cared for?'' Susannah shook her head. "I can't credit that, Del. Not after all these years.''

"He's been incarcerated for the last fifteen of them," Connor interjected. "In and out of prison on a regular basis prior to that, although I'm going by what I've been told. I haven't seen his criminal record yet." He shrugged. "How else to explain that post-card?''

"Unless it was sent by a Double B who needs your help," Tye murmured, almost to himself. "John Mac-Leish's body was never found, remember?''

Jess snorted. "For God's sake, when Del needed our help, did he send us a cryptic postcard that had us scratching our heads? No, he picked up the phone and called us. If this MacLeish was still alive and in trouble, why wouldn't he do the same?''

Tye smiled ruefully. "You're right, of course. I just don't like loose ends, and a supposed suicide who doesn't leave a body is a loose end in my book.''

"Maybe that loose end's been tied up in the inter-vening years," Connor said. "I can check into it, see if his death was ever solidly confirmed. But as much as I hate to, I've got to agree with Jess on this one, Tye. Your theory's a hard sell. Del's makes a kind of sense, if we go on the assumption that Jasper let his hatred of the Double B's fester all the years he was in prison. It's a starting point for the Bureau's inves-tigation into the late Mr. Scudder's motives, anyway.''

''You said Harmon rigged the bomb that—that—'' Susannah foundered, unsure of how to put her question. Del helped her out.

''That took my legs?'' His smile was wry. ''I've been without them now longer than I had them, sweetheart. It doesn't bother me like it used to, although I was pretty bitter for a long time afterward, which is why I let things like old friendships lapse. In the end a woman gave me back my sense of worth,'' he added quietly. ''But that's a story for another time.''

He sighed. ''We arrested Harmon, like I said. Brought him in, handed him over, and were told the Double B's were being disbanded. The official reason being that the war was winding down,'' he grimaced. ''The real one being that no one wanted us around anymore. So they split us up and started shipping us home, one by one. Your father was discharged first,'' he added to Susannah.

''How did Harmon rig a bomb when he was in custody?'' Jess asked dubiously.

''He didn't. He rigged it after he escaped and Mac-Leish and I were sent to bring him back.''

Del's tone was brisk, and Susannah had the feeling the briskness covered anger that had never really gone away. His next words seemed to prove her right.

''All of a sudden they remembered our existence when they realized they needed us for one last job. Harmon had the rep of being able to melt into the jungle like a ghost, and only another Double B stood a chance of recapturing him.'' He waved a weary hand. ''The rest is pretty boring. John and I took different trails, and by the luck of the draw I caught up with Zeke first. He pulled a gun, I shot first, and he fell. I started to walk toward him and I saw him lift his head and grin at me, just like he'd done a thousand times before when we were friends. And I knew. I knew even as my foot hit the ground that he'd set me up. They told me later that John dragged me out, fifteen miles on his back. He left Harmon's body there to be collected later, which it was.''

He pushed himself with an effort from his chair, steadying himself with his cane as he stood. He was still Greta's tough old mustang, Susannah thought with a pang, but reliving these memories had taken a lot out of him.

''If my theory about Jasper Scudder is right, sweetheart, I wish he'd come after me instead,'' he said, his voice sharp with regret. ''I'd have done anything to take the nightmare of these past nine months away from you. Thank God it's finally over.''

''That sounds like my cue,'' Jess said easily, reaching for the duffel bag beside him and getting to his feet. ''I've got a meeting later this afternoon,'' he explained. ''Besides, if I hang around any longer, I just know I'm going to be roped in to help give that ungrateful hoss its daily dose of antibiotics.''

His comment had the effect of lightening the moment, raising a dry chuckle even from Del. Jess always would lighten the mood, Susannah thought as he clapped Tye on the shoulder and dropped a quick kiss on her cheek before ruffling Danny's hair.

''Take care, you,'' he said sternly to her son. ''And you take care, too, Susannah,'' he added, his grin fading but the warmth in his eyes remaining. ''I'm glad I got the chance to know you.''

''Thanks for everything you did for me, Jess,'' she said softly. ''I'm glad we met, too.''

She would ask him to the wedding, she decided, as he and Del and Connor left the porch and crossed the yard. As with Del and Greta, Jess had been there for her during the darkest hours, and she wanted him to share her joy, too.

She hadn't realized she'd announced her intention out loud until Tye spoke.

''That's something we have to talk about, Suze.''

She shook her head. ''Uh-uh, Tye. The rule is that the wedding is the bride's big day, and she gets to make all the important decisions. Heavens, don't you know the groom's only there to even up the numbers?'' He was standing by the porch railing, and she smiled happily up at him. ''They're our friends. They should be at our—''

''Suze, I thought you understood.'' His tone was strained. ''I told you from the start I didn't believe in marriage. How could I, with Marvin's track record?''

He took a step toward her. ''But you've taught me to believe in love, honey,'' he said quietly. ''That's why I'm asking you to live with me. You make my world complete.''

The first thing she had to do was to get Danny safely into his carry-cot, Susannah told herself numbly. That was important. She had to concentrate on that. It was on the floor by her chair, and, holding her son to her with one arm, she bent slightly forward in her seat and reached for its handle.

Tye held out his arms. ''I'll hold—''

''*No!*''

He'd broken her concentration, she thought. Right

from the start the man had been breaking her concentration, scrambling her thoughts, clouding her judgment. But no more.

She secured Danny in the cot. Standing, she tucked her hair neatly behind her ears, and as she did the faint scent of French perfume touched the air.

When they'd first met, she'd told him she wished she could be someone other than who she really was. Until this very moment, she hadn't realized that she'd made her wish come true.

Sometime in the past few days she'd forgotten who Susannah Bird was—where she came from, what she stood for. It was time she remembered. It was time she went back to her own world.

"It would be forever, Suze. I *want* it to be forever. A piece of paper and a couple of sentences rattled off in front of a justice of the peace couldn't make what I feel for you any more real." His eyes were dark with entreaty. "I don't want you to be my first wife, don't you see? I want you to be the woman I love for the rest of my life."

The thing was, she thought, she still looked at him and saw an angel—a fallen angel, a being too beautiful and wonderful to belong to an ordinary woman like her. *I'll probably always remember you like that, Tye,* she told him silently. *You'll always be my weakness, and I'll never stop loving you. But I love my son, too. And I'll never be able to raise him as I was raised if I turn my back on everything I believe in.*

"It would be wrong."

She met his gaze calmly, and knew the strength she felt was a gift—possibly only a gift on loan, but for right now a much-needed gift. Danny had been a gift.

The friends she'd made here at the Double B had been gifts. She had been blessed with so much, Susannah told herself. She had no right to feel so bereft.

"We love each other, Suze. How can it be wrong when we love each other?" He was frowning, not in anger but in an obvious effort to understand.

And she couldn't make him understand. If he didn't know, nothing she could say would make it clear. She tried, anyway.

"It's wrong because we do love each other, Tye." She lifted Danny's carry-cot. She faced the man in front of her, and knew it would be for the last time.

"I know some folks figure that without that piece of paper it's free love. I think that piece of paper's the freedom part. When you take those vows and sign that paper you're throwing away all the conditions and all the safety nets—or you should be, if you go into it thinking that way."

She furrowed her brow thoughtfully. "Maybe that's where Marvin went wrong. Maybe even with seven marriages under his belt, he never really felt like he was married at all. You're not your daddy, Tye. You should have trusted yourself."

She looked away. "Paul Johnson's going into Last Chance to pick up some feed. I believe I'll hitch a ride into town with him and ask him to drop me and Danny off at the bus station. I've been away from Fox Hollow for too long. I think I'd like to show my son where his roots are."

"For God's sake, Susannah!" The words sounded wrenched from him. "I'm not just going to stand here and watch you walk out of my—"

Calmness fled. "That's *exactly* what I want you to

do, Tyler!'' she said with shaky intensity. ''I want you
to let me go while I still can—because if I end up
staying, if I end up living with you in California without a ring on my finger, everything you say you love
about me will…will…'' Her throat closed. She felt
hot wetness on her cheeks.

''Hell, Suze.'' His arms were around her, his words
murmured against her hair. ''We can work this out
somehow. You know we can. Let's go inside and talk
this over.''

Just for a moment she let herself breathe in the scent
of him. It would work out, she thought. It would work
out because she wouldn't be able to stay strong, it
would work out because she wouldn't be able to face
losing him, it would work out because all he would
have to do was ask her one more time and she'd give
in.

It would work out. And it would still be wrong.

She took a deep breath. ''Del needs your help with
the horse.''

He made an impatient gesture. ''Forget that, honey.
It's more important that we—''

''I know. But right now I think I'd like a few
minutes to myself, Tye.'' She forced a shaky smile to
her lips, and met his unconvinced gaze. ''It's been a
pretty unsettling week for me, and I'm not even sure
I've taken it in yet that Scudder's dead. Finding out
on top of everything else that I jumped to the wrong
conclusion about how it was going to be between you
and me…'' She swallowed. ''Like I said, I need some
time alone right now. We'll talk when you get back
to the house, okay?''

Slippery slope, Granny Lacey, she thought, holding

her breath as Tye hesitated. *But it's to save me from an even more slippery one.*

"Okay, Suze." His expression was troubled. He looked at Danny, now blinking drowsily at them from his carry-cot. "You want me to give you a hand putting Dan the Man down for his nap first?"

"I—I don't think so, Tye." Her voice sounded almost normal, Susannah noted, which was quite an achievement, given that she felt as if she was being torn in two. "He's halfway there already."

He nodded. He jammed his hands irresolutely into his back pockets. He saw her watching him, and a corner of his mouth lifted wryly as he turned away and walked to the end of the porch.

"I also told you I didn't believe in miracles." He stopped and looked at her as he spoke, his eyes so dark she couldn't read the expression in them. "I do now, Suze. You're my miracle," he said quietly.

She waited until he'd reached the yard and was heading toward the bunkhouse before she answered him, her response barely audible.

"And you were my miracle, Tye." Her vision blurred. In the shimmer of her tears she saw a tall, broad-shouldered man with hair the color of burnished gold. "You always will be," she whispered.

She couldn't risk saying goodbye to Del, Susannah thought as she hurried into her bedroom and packed Danny's essentials and her few belongings into the battered suitcase she'd been living out of for so long. It was rude, it was unforgivable, but she just couldn't trust herself to carry it off without dissolving into tears.

She would write him as soon as she could to let

him know how much finding and getting to know her father's friend had meant to her, she promised herself as she sped into the yard and saw Paul Johnson heading for his truck.

To her relief, Johnson asked no awkward questions when she approached him with her request. With his usual economy of words he merely nodded, tossed her single suitcase easily into the back of the truck, and helped her get Danny securely into his infant seat. His keen gaze sharpened at the tearstains on her cheeks, and he grunted.

"I take it you're looking to put some miles between you and this place. You know there isn't a bus out of Last Chance until tomorrow, don't you, Miz Barrett?"

Susannah stared at him, appalled. "Are you sure?" At his nod she fumbled in her purse for her pocketbook. "I'd better see if I have enough money to take a room for the night, then," she said worriedly, but even as she spoke he started the vehicle.

"No, you hang on to your money, ma'am. I can take you into Leetown and you can catch a Greyhound there. It's about an hour's drive, though, so you might as well get a little shut-eye if you can," he added gruffly. "Looks to me like you could use some."

She didn't need sleep, Susannah thought as she stared unseeingly out of the truck's passenger-side window. Sleep meant dreams. What she really needed was to be able to shut off her brain completely for a time. *Except at some point you'd have to turn it back on,* she told herself dully. *Too bad brainwashing doesn't mean what a body might figure it did. That would be the way—take it to the laundry and get it back all spanking clean with the memories removed.*

"He let you down, did he?"

With a start Susannah realized that the usually tac-
iturn man beside her had spoken, and with an even
greater start she saw that they were already passing
Last Chance and turning down a sideroad smaller than
the secondary highway they'd been on. She bit her
lip, reluctant to discuss her hasty departure from the
Double B, but feeling she owed the man who was
making that departure possible some explanation.

"Tye didn't let me down. I let myself down," she
said softly. "I tried to become someone I'm not, and
I guess that never works out."

Beside her Johnson pursed his lips, gearing the
truck down and turning again on to a graveled road.
He saw her slightly puzzled glance and shrugged.

"It's a trade-off, Miz Barrett. Twenty miles of good
road or seven bad. This truck's got heavy-duty everything, so I figured we'd cut some distance off the trip.
But getting back to what you just said—I don't know
as I agree with you there."

He shook his head. "You can change yourself into
anyone you want if you've got a strong enough reason
for doing it. Kind of like that Skinwalker legend."

"Except Skinwalker's reasons are evil ones," she
replied distractedly. The road had narrowed to little
more than a trail, and ahead of them it took a steep
incline. She turned to look at Danny in the seat behind, and saw he was fast asleep. "And despite what
Alice Tahe says, no one really believes in shape-
shifters and ghosts, do they?"

"I do." His craggy features briefly relaxed into a
smile at her startled look. "Not literally," he added
laconically. "But the past can haunt a man, and if you

want an example of that you don't have to look further than Hawkins. I don't know what he went through in 'Nam but he's got his demons, that's for sure.''

Del's story wasn't hers to tell, Susannah thought, and even if it had been, she didn't really feel much like talking. It was obvious that Johnson was making an effort to take her mind off her problems, but despite her earlier fantasy of erasing all memory of Tye, thinking about him was a way of holding on to him for a little longer.

You could be holding on to him for real, a small voice in her head said. *You could tell Johnson you've changed your mind and ask him to turn the truck around right now. Tye loves you, so, like he said, what difference does a piece of paper make to that love?*

Maybe to another woman it wouldn't make any difference at all, Susannah told herself sadly. But to her it did. It had to. She couldn't just pick and choose among her beliefs for the ones that didn't inconvenience her.

It sounded good, she thought a heartbeat later. Everything she'd just been going over in her mind sounded good, sounded convincing. It was all a lie.

He'd wanted to talk it out. She'd had the chance to fight for what she believed in. But her pride had gotten in the way.

You figured the man should have felt the same way you do about making it legal. You were afraid of having it out with him, and still not changing his mind. For heaven's sake, Susannah Bird—the plain, unvarnished truth of the matter is you were too darn proud to fight for the love of your life!

''...might have been different for Del if he'd had a

pretty young wife to come home to like your daddy did. Still, I guess Daniel's had more than a few of his own demons to battle over the years.''

Johnson's tone was musingly thoughtful, and for a moment what he'd said didn't catch Susannah's attention any more than the rest of what he'd obviously been saying had. Then it clicked, and she jerked her gaze to him.

''What did you say?''

He steered the truck around a deep rut before he answered. ''Del. I figure things might have been easier for the man if he'd had someone—''

''No.'' Her body knew, Susannah thought faintly. She could feel the icy sweat trickling down her spine, and a giant hand seemed to be wrapping itself around her chest, making it hard to breathe. Her body knew, even if her mind wasn't allowing her to accept it yet.

''No, Mr. Johnson, not that. You said something about my father. You talked about him as if he was still alive.''

''Alive and due to be released from West Virginia Correctional in a couple of days.'' He brought the truck to a halt, and turned to her. ''He's been in prison all these years. I know he made your granny promise not to tell you he got sent up for murder.''

''You're wrong.'' Her lips felt almost too numb to form the words. ''Daniel Bird died fifteen years ago. He died when I was just a little girl, not long after my mama passed away.''

Passed away from what? You told Tye it was from the fever, but Granny Lacey never actually came out and said so, did she? And you never pressed her on it...because even though you were only a little girl,

*you knew the terrible things that had been done to
her, and how she had died. You knew that Lacey Bird,
who couldn't countenance the whitest of tiny white
lies, would have lied a hundred times over to have
saved her granddaughter from such a nightmarish
truth.*

"Slippery slope, Granny Lacey," she murmured
unevenly. "And you slid down it willingly, just to
shield me from the pain."

"No, Miz Bird, my *brother* died fifteen years ago,"
the man beside her corrected her. "The same day the
charges against him of raping and murdering Jessica
Bird were thrown out on a technicality, Dwight
walked out of court and straight into the bullet your
daddy fired through his heart. I know, because I was
in court that day too…except my conviction was up-
held."

Now her mind had caught up with her body, Susannah thought fearfully. In horror she studied the
craggy features, the triumphantly amused gaze of the
man she'd called Paul Johnson. Those big hands—
workingman's hands, she'd thought once, workingman's hands with heavy rawboned strength in the
wrists—were killer's hands. She fixed her eyes on the
horsehair bracelet encircling one of them, because she
didn't want to watch his face when he answered her.

"Who *are* you?" she whispered hoarsely.

Her body knew. Her mind knew. But she still
needed to hear him say it.

"Jasper Scudder, Miz Susannah Bird." His smile
grew. "And I've been waiting for this moment for a
long, long time."

Chapter Fifteen

"That should do you for today," Tye grunted, stepping away from the gelding. Peeling a pair of washleather gloves from his hands, he slapped them against his thigh to remove the dust before tucking them into a back pocket.

"Look at the marks on that hind quarter there," Del muttered in disgust. "I've let things go around here these past few months, dammit. Time was when nothing happened on this ranch that I didn't know about."

"Yeah, you're slacking off, old man," Tye said dryly. "You think it might have something to do with the fact that you've been a little preoccupied lately with trying to find out who was trying to shut the Double B down?"

"Maybe." Del squinted at the gelding. "But it chafes at me that I didn't see what Bradley was. I should be thinking of turning this place over to a younger man one of these days, Tye. You interested?"

His question was offhandedly casual, Tye noted, but it still put him in the position of having to turn his former mentor down. He cleared his throat.

"I don't think so, Del." He rubbed a thumb along

his jawline. "I've got as much as I can handle with the bodyguard business out in California. Security's pretty lucrative nowadays."

"So you're getting rich, big deal." Del raised an eyebrow. "You're not happy, Adams, and I know it. You practically jumped at the chance to come back here when I called to ask for your help."

"I wasn't happy, no," Tye retorted shortly. "But now I've got a shot at it."

"A shot at it?" Del's gaze narrowed. "With Susannah? For God's sake, I thought you had a sure thing going there, boy, not just a shot at it. How'd you manage to blow it?"

And this was the man who figured he was out of touch with what was going on around him, Tye thought with brief irritation. He resisted the urge to tell Hawkins to butt out.

"We had a little misunderstanding a few minutes ago. I've got some fences to mend with her when I get back to the house."

"She figured marriage. You wanted to shack up with her. Was that the misunderstanding?" Del's phrasing was crudely blunt, and it touched off a spark in Tye.

"Back the hell away from that one, Hawkins, or so help me I'll—" He stopped, not wanting to complete the threat. Del's smile was hard.

"You'll what, California? Kick my ass? You tried to, once, and you never even landed a single punch, remember?"

For a long moment the two men stared at each other. Then Tye felt the anger inside him deflate. He managed a lopsided grin.

"Yeah, Susannah figured marriage, and I..." He lifted his shoulders. "Well, I just don't see myself as the marrying kind, Del. You know that."

"I know you've always said you didn't believe in the institution." Del's tone was quieter, too. "That from everything you'd seen it was just a business contract, and like any contract, made to be broken. That doesn't really explain why you wouldn't go through with it just to please her if that's what she had her heart set on." He frowned. "Unless you don't love her. Is that it?"

"Love her?" A vision of the way she'd looked two nights ago flashed through Tye's mind—wet hair, wet lips, the silk robe he'd given her slipping from creamy skin. He bit back a groan. "That little lady's got my heart for good," he said huskily. "She knows she has. That's why I don't understand why the rest of it matters a damn."

"Because she's Susannah Bird, and she was brought up to believe in things like marriage and vows," Del said quietly. "And because she's not a coward. Too bad you are, Adams."

Tye jerked his head up and met the other man's assessing stare. "You can call me a lot of names, Del, but that's not one of them. What the hell am I supposed to be scared of?"

"Of losing her." Del picked up his cowboy hat from a nearby hay bale. "You think signing a marriage certificate is the first step toward signing divorce papers. Hell, I don't know as I blame you, what with your father's track record and the musical-chair marriages you see out there in Hollywood. So you figure as long as you don't marry her you've got a chance of holding on to her.''

He sighed. ''What you never understood was that you didn't grow up in the real world, Tye. You don't live in the real world now. You live in La-La Land, like Connor said. Susannah's a real woman, and she wants the real deal.''

Tye felt as if the physical confrontation that had threatened to erupt a few minutes ago between him and the man standing in front of him had actually happened, and that he'd just taken a roundhouse kick somewhere in the area of his solar plexus. He sat down heavily on a bale, for a moment unable to catch his breath.

It was true, he thought dizzily. All his big talk about not believing in marriage was just that—talk. Del was right, dammit. He was *scared*.

He was scared of losing her, scared of waking up one day and finding a note on the pillow next to him, scared of going back to living in a world that didn't include Susannah Bird, that didn't include the child she'd named after him.

He'd been so scared he'd come close to making all his fears a reality.

Sweat had popped out on his forehead, he realized shakily. He felt as if he'd been walking blindfolded toward the edge of a cliff, and had ripped the blindfold off just in time to save himself from taking that last fatal step.

''She wants you to give her away,'' he said hoarsely. Slowly he got to his feet, and met Del's keen gaze. ''I guess that means I'll have to find someone else for my best man, right?''

"I can't walk the bride down the aisle and be standing beside a nervous groom at the same time, buddy," Del said with a smile as he hefted a saddle with one hand and grasped his cane with the other. "You're going to have to find—"

He broke off as the wall-mounted phone beside Tye rang shrilly. The gelding in the nearby stall whickered.

"It only comes through to the barn if no one's picked up at the house by the third ring," Del said testily. "I know Susannah wouldn't answer it, and Connor's in my study waiting for a fax he requested from the Bureau. Hit the speaker button, would you, Tye? Ten to one it's someone trying to sell me something."

If it was, Tye thought a second later as the operator's nasal tones came on the line, the salesman certainly had moxie.

"Collect call for a Mr. Delbert Hawkins. Will you accept?"

"Probably not," Del growled. "Who's calling?"

"Collect call from West Virginia for a Mr. Hawkins, sir. The caller won't give his—" The operator paused. When she spoke again her annoyance was audible even over the poor line. "The caller says to tell you he was a double bee. He says you'll know what that means."

Del's face was ashen, Tye saw in alarm. But even as he stepped swiftly to his side to relieve him of the heavy saddle the ex-marine waved him away.

"Put—put him through, operator."

His face was carved in grim lines as he waited for the voice on the other end to speak. Tye realized his own jaw was painfully clenched and with an effort he relaxed it…only to have it drop open in shock as Del's mystery caller spoke, his drawling tones a masculine but tellingly similar version of his daughter's.

"Don't use my name, ol' buddy. Could be there's folks listening in on my end, and I don't aim to give them no ammo to use against me. You know who you talkin' to, Del?''

"I—I know who I'm talking to.'' Del's throat worked. "I was told you were dead.''

"Closest thing to it for the last fifteen years,'' Daniel Bird said softly. "I didn't want to bring any more shame on my loved ones than I had to, so I went along with the suggestion that it was best folks believed that. Who'd you hear it from?''

"From a young woman you're going to have to do a lot of explaining to,'' Del said cautiously.

"I figured her granny had passed on when the letters stopped. Thank the Lord she knew to come to you.'' There was shaky relief in Bird's voice, but almost immediately it was replaced by desperate urgency. "She's in danger, Del. I thought I'd be out in time to tell you in person. That's why I sent you the card—so it wouldn't be such a shock.''

"I got it. It was one hell of a shock in itself.''

"I didn't know no other way to warn you, and as it turned out they delayed my release date for a week, anyway. You're going to have to look after her for me until I can get there, so listen real careful. There's a man by the name of Jasper Scudder, means to do her harm. He'll be getting out of the joint in a day or two, and I reckon the first thing he'll do is go a'huntin' for my—''

"He must have got early release.'' For the first time

Tye spoke. "He's been hunting her for the better part of a year now, but his hunting days are over. Scudder's dead."

"No, he's not."

Turning quickly, Tye saw Connor standing in the doorway of the barn. Over the speaker-phone came Bird's alarmed voice.

"Who's there, Del? What's this about Jasper?"

"They're friends, old buddy," Del reassured him. He turned to Connor. "What do you mean, Scudder's not dead?"

"I mean it looks like that driver's license was planted by the burned body of your former hired hand, Kevin Bradley," Connor said heavily. "But the picture on it was a forgery. The Bureau faxed the real Jasper Scudder's picture through to me a minute ago. This is the bastard we've got to watch for."

Of course, Tye thought with leaden certainty. Connor hadn't met the ranch's other employee yet. Even as his fearful glance confirmed the familiar features of Paul Johnson on the photo Connor held out to Del he was racing from the barn, a terrible knowledge screaming through his mind. And when he burst into the house calling out her name, some part of him knew not to expect an answer.

I'll hitch a ride into town with him and ask him to drop me and Danny off at the bus station....

She'd walked out of his life...and straight into the arms of her killer.

"LAST NIGHT you shot your own kin in cold blood to save my life." Susannah tried to still the tremor in her voice. "Why didn't you let Lyle kill me then, instead of going to the trouble of bringing me and my son out here to do the same thing?''

In the light of the gas-mantle lantern, Johnson's— she corrected herself—Scudder's shadow wavered fantastically against the damp stone of the cave. Again she corrected herself. It was a cavern. On their trek into it from where he'd hidden the truck he'd told her there was a difference.

''Most folks don't know or don't care. Me, I like to find things out. This here's a cavern because you got to take these twisty ol' passageways to get to it. Hellfire, Miz Bird, watch that baby's head.''

He'd been prodding her from behind with his gun, the miner's lamp attached to the hard hat he was wearing beaming a harsh white light over her shoulder. He hadn't listened to her earlier pleas to leave Danny in the truck, where her son had a chance of being found.

She was going to die. She could accept that, Susannah thought as Scudder unrolled the bedroll he'd brought with him. She could even accept that he didn't intend to kill her right away, and although her mind wanted to shy away from it, she forced herself to acknowledge the use to which her captor meant to put that same bedroll.

But she couldn't accept that her baby was going to die, too. She wouldn't accept it, she told herself with numb determination. Whatever it took, she wouldn't allow that to happen.

''I didn't let Lyle kill you for the same reason I didn't let myself kill you a dozen times over since you started running from me,'' Scudder said. Frowning, he sat down on the bedroll before getting up again and moving it slightly to one side. ''Because that wasn't the way I planned it. Oh, me giving myself a tap on the head and then being the hero who blew him away was in my plan, although Lyle didn't know it. I only came up with that when it looked like I needed to throw Adams and the rest off my trail for a little longer. Same with that hothead Bradley, who was only too eager to agree to meet me later last night when I let him think I was just as pissed off at Hawkins as he was.''

He shook his head. ''But when you spend fifteen years with nothing else to think about, you've got a pretty solid idea of what you want when the time finally comes. I wanted you scared. I wanted you scared for a long time. And when I found out you were expectin', little mama, I felt like it was Christmas and my birthday all rolled into one.''

He glanced her way, and the flat sheen of his eyes chilled her. She hugged a blanket-swathed Danny closer to her, glad that he had fallen into a light nap.

''Daniel Bird's gonna know his daughter didn't just die the same way his pretty wife did, but that she was in fear for months beforehand, too. And he's going to lose the grandson he never had a chance to hold.''

Her father was alive. How many times as a little girl had she wished for exactly that? Susannah wondered. And now that she knew it was so, she wished for Daniel Bird's sake that he really had been dead for all these years. He was due out of prison any time now, Scudder had told her. Daniel Bird would rejoin the world only to find that what remained of his share in it had been savagely destroyed by one of the men who'd torn it apart once before.

''Why'd you do my mama like you did?'' The

question burst from her with agonized intensity. "What did Jessica Bird ever do to you and your brother Dwight that you had to behave worse than beasts to her and then kill her?"

"She walked by us." Lying back on the bedroll, Scudder grinned. "We were in the parking lot of a market, looking in vehicles to see if any fool woman had left her purse lying around. Dwight and me had been working the mines, but we'd been laid off for about three months by then," he added as an aside.

"Anyway, she passed by on the way to her own car, and Dwight gave me a look. I knew he was thinking neither one of us had gotten any lovin' from the ladies since we'd hit hard times, and here was a real sweet one purely dropped into our laps. We got to her before she started up her car, told her to drive out to the old river road, and just did what came natural. It was an accident she was killed, you know."

He shrugged. "She tried to get away from Dwight. Slipped and hit her head on a rock. Dwight was tore up about it for a time, felt a little guilty."

Nausea rose in her and she closed her eyes. "You were caught and put on trial," she said, her voice a thin sliver. "And Dwight got off."

"My little brother got off," Scudder agreed. "I disremember all the fancy lawyer talk but there was something wrong with the evidence against him, and me they could only get on the rape. Your daddy went crazy in the courtroom."

"But then he went home and got his gun," Susannah said softly. "He was raised to believe in justice. When the system couldn't deliver it he took it into his own hands, and he ended up going to prison for a longer sentence than the one his wife's killer got.''

A corner of Danny's blanket had slipped aside. In the act of adjusting it, Susannah felt her breath catch in her throat with alarm.

Her baby's body temperature was falling dangerously. Already there was a coolness to his skin, and his breathing seemed shallower than it had been. She hugged him closer, her mind working furiously.

''I was raised that way, too.'' Scudder hadn't seemed to notice her distraction. ''I swore I'd make him pay for killing Dwight. Figured I'd go for the old lady first and then come after his little girl. I talked a little too free about it to a cellmate, though.''

''Frank.''

The man who'd so briefly been her husband hadn't been in time to save Granny Lacey, Susannah thought. But Frank Barrett had given his life in an attempt to protect her, as she now intended to give hers to protect the child they'd made in their one night together.

''Barrett.'' Scudder exhaled. ''Just my bad luck he'd bunked for a time with Daniel before transferring to the prison I was in. Seems your granny had been sending letters and pictures to her jailbird son all those years, and when Daniel became friends with Frank he showed him your photo. Some men need a dream to hang on to when they're behind bars, and I guess you became Frank's. When he realized I had my own dreams for you, he told me he was going to rat me out.''

He sighed. ''Two packs of smokes should buy a man a hit, not a miss. At least Frank being laid up in the prison hospital gave me a head start on him when

I got early release.'' He closed one eye in a wink. ''Clean livin' and good behavior. The parole board figured I'd paid my debt to society.''

Without warning he got to his feet. ''Party time, sweetness.''

She needed a few more minutes, Susannah thought urgently. While Scudder had been talking she'd been trying desperately to come up with a plan, and she'd finally hit upon the only course of action that had any chance of success.

Success didn't mean she was going to leave this dank underground chamber alive, she told herself steadily. Success meant her son wouldn't perish with her.

She wasn't ever going to see Tye again.

She'd been holding that thought at bay since the moment Scudder had revealed his identity and she'd known she was doomed. Now Susannah let it flood over her.

A fallen angel. That was how he'd appeared to her the first time, and that was how she wanted to hold him now in her mind, she thought—glowing and burnished by the sun, radiating heat and life. Just for a second the shadows around her seemed to be touched with some warmth, some golden light.

He'd loved her. He'd loved the child he'd helped bring into the world. Like an arrow piercing her heart, terrible pain lanced through her.

Scudder made an impatient sound. ''Put your little'un down, mama, and let's get started. I fooled them all the way along the line, but more'n likely the feds have figured things out by now. Hell, even a blind sow digs up an acorn once in a while.''

He had the sin of pride, Susannah thought suddenly. Perhaps she could use it against him.

"Waylon and Lyle fooled them, you mean," she said dismissively. She squatted down and placed Danny in the carry-cot by her feet, tucking the blankets around him with care until only his face peeked out. She ran a tender finger along one delicately perfect eyebrow, knowing it was the last time she would ever touch the son she loved more than life itself.

Then she stood up, deliberately turning her back on Scudder and peering around the floor of the cavern as if looking for a suitable spot for the carry-cot. She didn't even look at him as she spoke.

"They were the killers, and if you hadn't turned on your own blood kin Lyle would have gotten clean away. The law'll be looking for you, Scudder, but you weren't their first pick of the litter. The Lynds boys were."

He stared flatly at her and his hand went to the butt of the gun stuck in his belt. She held her breath, hoping she hadn't prompted him into action too soon.

"I didn't call on Waylon and Lyle till I had to. I needed them to keep you on the run while I got myself established in the very place I knew you'd run to," he said with quiet venom. "I told you I'd had years to work out my plan. You think I didn't know everything there was to know about Daniel Bird when I was through, including the name of the one man he trusted completely, the man his daughter would have been told she could trust, too?"

He shrugged, and to her relief some of the hair-trigger tension seemed to drain from him. "A place like the Double B can always use an extra hand. I got myself hired on with some forged references, and then I just sat back and waited. When Adams showed up with his story about finding and losing some woman who'd just given birth by the side of the road, I knew my waiting had paid off.''

"You heard secondhand about Danny's birth?" Just for a moment she was diverted. "You weren't watching from somewhere nearby?"

To her amazement, she saw that her question had shaken him, and she took the opportunity to place the carry-cot in the spot her frantic gaze had been searching for, and had finally found. In the corner by one solid wall of the cavern was a grouping of three large boulders. They were set so they enclosed a roughly triangular space, and it was inside that protected triangle that she deposited the carry-cot.

Scudder's expression was closed. "I told you, the first I knew you'd shown up was when Adams tried to get the sheriff to mount a search for a missing woman and a baby," he muttered, bending down to pick up the lantern. "I've gone by that area a dozen times since and it's desert, without an inch of cover a man could conceal himself behind. You don't know what you're talking about, lady."

"But you do, don't you?"

Susannah heard the dawning horror in her voice. She saw an unwilling shadow of the same emotion flicker across Scudder's set features.

"You met him, didn't you? You met him and you sold your soul to him in return for his help, just like Vincent Rosario did," she said tightly. "How did you know I was at Greta's that night when even Tye and Del weren't aware she'd taken me in? No one *could* have known—unless they were there in the desert, watching when she hitched up my car and drove away with me and Danny.''

She took a step toward Scudder. ''Rosario said Skinwalker had come back. He said he wanted the baby—*my* baby. That's the deal you made with him, isn't it? When you're finished here with me you're going to hand my son over to him!''

Chapter Sixteen

"You're out of your mind." Scudder fumbled at his belt for his gun. Clumsily he drew it out and pointed it at her. "Skinwalker's a legend, dammit—a bogeyman. He doesn't exist."

"That's what you've been telling yourself," Susannah said thinly. "And maybe he made it easy for you to tell yourself that. Did he come to you in the darkness one night when you were standing guard at the Double B gate? Was he just a voice over the telephone, offering to help you in return for you getting him what he wanted?"

"I've heard enough, goddammit," Scudder said thickly. "Whether I made a deal with someone or not, I don't want to hear any more of this Skinwalker business. Get over to that bedroll, lady, or I'll—"

"*He's not getting my son, Scudder!*"

Even as his hand clamped around her wrist, Susannah launched herself at him. For a second he was taken off guard. In the wavering light of the lantern she saw his face contort into a mask of hate, saw him bring the gun up, saw his finger tighten on the trigger.

And although in the days to come she persuaded

herself it had been her imagination, for a moment she was sure she saw *two* hideously elongated shadows on the cavern wall grappling with her, where there should have been only Scudder's.

Her arm came up at the same second that he pulled the trigger. His shot went wide.

"You little bitch," he grunted. "I like 'em feisty but you're just—"

Abruptly he broke off. Susannah saw his eyes narrow as he recognized the sound she'd already heard and identified.

From somewhere in the deeper reaches of the cavern came an ominous rumbling. Overlying it was a second sound—a high-pitched squeaking that seemed to be gathering rapidly toward them from every direction.

She was a country girl, Susannah thought in weary satisfaction. She'd known the bats would come flooding out first, and in a cavern this size there would be thousands of them. Even if Scudder started running now they would impede his progress enough that the approaching rockfall would overtake him long before he got to safety.

And God willing, Danny would be safe in his enclosure of boulders until the search parties reached him.

"You're about as dumb as butter, Mr. Jasper Scudder," she said softly. "You once working the mines and all, a body would think you'd know better'n to go firing off a gun in a place like this. While you're running, you might want to remember some names to keep your mind off how you're going to die. Names like Frank Barrett's."

The rumbling was getting louder. Scudder looked wildly down the yawning mouth of the cavern and then back toward the way they'd come in.

"You're going to die, too," he snarled. He crammed the miner's hat on his head. "Don't you get it, you crazy bitch? You're going to die, too!"

"Nick Stephanopoulos," Susannah said, but already Scudder had whirled desperately around and was heading for the narrow passageway. She saw the light on his hard hat bobbing eerily for a few feet, and then it disappeared as he turned the corner.

A sudden shower of rock chips rained down on her. The high-pitched squeaking rose in volume. Calmly Susannah walked over to the lantern and blew it out. In the darkness she felt her way to the tight triangle of boulders and curled up beside them, content to be this close to her son even if she couldn't reach through to touch him.

"Lacey and Jessica Bird," she whispered, ending the list of Scudder's victims. "Granny? Mama? You keep watch over my little boy, you hear me? There'll be folks come looking for us pretty soon. You lead them to him."

Suddenly the velvet blackness was filled with the sound of rushing wings and twittering calls, hundreds upon hundreds of them, speeding toward safety. They were God's creatures, she thought, and like all He'd created they'd been given their own gifts. They knew she was there and as long as she stayed still they wouldn't fly into her.

She should say a prayer, she supposed. But maybe He would understand if her last thoughts were of a fallen angel, and the brief slice of heaven she'd known on this earth.

"I love you, Tye," she whispered. The rumbling got louder, and now the very earth around her was shaking. The crashing filled her ears and all around her the cavern's roof began falling as the last of the bats streamed past. She closed her eyes and saw a tanned face, eyes as blue as the sky smiling down at her. "I'll always love—"

"Susannah!"

Her eyes flew open in shock. Light flooded the cavern—light from the electric lantern Tye was holding in one hand.

"Tye!"

She had to be in heaven already, she told herself faintly. But heaven was supposed to have pearly gates and music and—

"Suze, thank God!" He raced to her and pulled her to her feet. "Where's Danny?" Raw fear sharpened his already edged tone.

"He—he's here, Tye." Dazedly she began to lift the carry-cot from the enclosing shield of boulders, but he stopped her.

"Just pick him up and let's go, Suze." Another piece of the ceiling crashed down a few feet away. "There's a second passageway out of here. If we hurry we've got a—"

The ground shuddered underfoot, and to Susannah's horror she saw the very walls around them start to buckle. Even as she reached for Danny, Tye scooped him up, his face grim.

"This way, Suze. *Hurry!*"

Forever after, she found it hard to recall much at

all of that hellish race through the bowels of the earth. But Tye seemed to know each twist and turn of the corridor as if he'd explored every inch of it dozens of times in the past, and at some point, the dank mushroom smell that had permeated her nostrils since Scudder had forced her to enter the cavern began to mingle with another, achingly familiar scent.

That scent was fresh air, Susannah realized. And the light around them was no longer coming from the lantern, but from sunshine shafting through an opening just ahead. Tears blurred her vision as she clambered up onto solid ground before reaching back to take Danny from Tye's uplifted arms.

She chafed at the tiny hands. Danny opened his eyes sleepily. He blinked against the sunlight and scowled.

''Is he all right, Suze?'' Tye was beside her, his face drawn. She nodded, unable at first to speak.

''He—he seems just fine, Tye.'' She turned tear-washed eyes to his. ''How did you find us? How did you even know where to look?''

He pushed a strand of hair back from her temple. Instead of answering her question, he let his hand continue moving to the back of her neck. It settled there. She felt his fingers gently gather in a palmful of her hair.

''Just let me look at you for a moment, honey.'' His voice was uneven. ''I was so afraid I'd—'' A muscle moved visibly at the side of his jaw. ''Oh, Suze, I was so damned afraid I was going to be too late,'' he whispered.

''Tye.'' Wonderingly she touched a wind-burnished

cheekbone. A single silvery track ran down it. "Tye, you—you're *crying*."

"You and Danny." His smile was tight. "You're my everything. My *everything,* Suze, do you understand? And I came so close to losing you."

He looked away for a second, and took a deep breath. Then he looked back at her. "Your father's alive, Susannah."

Tremulously she nodded. "I know. Scudder—" Just saying the name brought nausea to her throat. "Scudder told me. He told me everything."

Even as the words passed her lips doubt assailed her. What exactly *had* Scudder said in those final few minutes—or more importantly, what had he actually admitted to? Suddenly she felt as if she was awakening from a nine-month-long bad dream, a bad dream that had culminated in that feverish and already jumbled confrontation between her and the man who'd hunted her down.

The accusations she'd leveled at him near the end had been part of that fantastical and twisted confrontation in the shadows, Susannah thought slowly. Under a sunlit sky they seemed ridiculously far-fetched. Scudder had been more than evil enough to have masterminded his own cruel schemes without the help of a bogeyman that didn't—*couldn't*—exist.

"Then the FBI are going to need to talk to you, honey, because Jasper himself isn't going to be available for questioning." Tye squinted across the canyon. "See that?"

She looked in the direction he'd indicated. Except for an agitated flock of birds darting around in the air, there was nothing of note there as far as she could tell.

"See what?" she asked, confused.

"That's just it. There's nothing there to see," he said quietly. "Scudder's truck is behind that outcrop of rock higher up. There should be an entranceway to the cavern there, but it's gone."

They weren't birds, they were bats, she realized belatedly. They'd made it out. Jasper Scudder hadn't. Right now all she could manage to feel at that knowledge was overwhelming relief.

"Daniel phoned Del just after you left." Tye grimaced wryly. "Very long story, honey, and you'll hear it all when we get back to the ranch. But when we realized Johnson was Scudder and he had you and Danny, Connor asked your father if there was anything he could tell us about the man that might give us a clue as to where he'd taken you. Daniel said something about Scudder having worked in a mine at one time. I thought there was an outside chance he might have come here, and when I found his truck I knew I'd guessed right. Then I felt the cave-in begin."

He squeezed his eyes shut. When he opened them again Susannah saw raw pain sheening his gaze.

"Del had always forbidden us to explore these caverns, so naturally I got to know them like the back of my hand." He shook his head. "I died a thousand deaths on my way in, honey. If I hadn't found you and Danny when I did I'd still be in there searching for you."

"You keep saving me, Tye," she said softly.

He shook his head. "No, Suze. You saved me.

That's why I don't want you to come out to California and live with me.''

She stared at him. A body didn't have to be in a cavern to be shut off from all light, all warmth, she realized shakily. It wasn't necessary to be caught in a cave-in to feel suddenly as if the very ground beneath your feet was about to give way.

"You don't?" Her throat closed on the question.

"I don't." He held her gaze. "I want you right here with me in New Mexico, honey. I'm going to be running the Double B with Del from now on." Brief uncertainty shadowed his features. "Do you think you'd like being a rancher's wife, Suze?"

"I think I'd *love* being a rancher's wife, Tye," she whispered, pure joy spreading through her. Answering joy turned the indigo gaze holding hers to a blue that looked as if it had been stolen from heaven. Tye brought his mouth to hers in a kiss that was almost a vow.

"You, me and Dan the Man, Suze," he said finally, lifting his head. A corner of his mouth quirked upward as he took her son from her and pulled her to her feet. "A Harley isn't the most practical choice of transportation for the three of us. Do you think my bad-boy biker days are over?"

"I think your biker days are over," she said promptly. "Danny's new daddy's going to be lookin' for a minivan, Tye." She raised herself on her tiptoes and planted a kiss square on his mouth. "But it wouldn't be the Double B if there wasn't a little bit of bad in its boys."

Lovingly Susannah gazed at the big man holding the tiny baby, and felt her heart overflow.

"Let's go home now, Tye," she said softly. "Let's go home to the Double B."

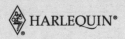

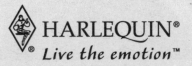

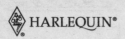

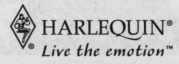

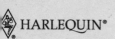

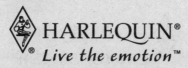

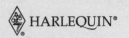

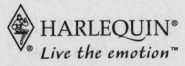